DEADLY INHERITANCE

"This is the TV room," Vicki told Andrew, a few minutes later.

The room had a wide-screen TV with surround sound speakers, a stereo video and a satellite decoder. There were two comfy-looking sofas. There was even a small gas fire, which Andrew switched on.

"Daddy likes his comforts," Vicki said. "What do you want to watch?"

"Why don't we see what's on?" Andrew suggested.

Vicki pressed a button on the TV and immediately, before the picture appeared, there was a loud, ear-piercing scream which seemed to come from the back of the room.

"Amazing sound," Andrew said.

"That wasn't the TV!" Vicki shouted, rushing to the door. "That was my mother!"

Other titles by David Belbin in the Point Crime series:

Avenging Angel
Break Point
Final Cut
Shoot the Teacher
The Beat: Missing Person
The Beat: Black and Blue

Coming soon in Point Crime:

The Beat: Smokescreen
David Belbin

The Alibi
Malcolm Rose

POINT CRIME

DEADLY INHERITANCE

David Belbin

SCHOLASTIC

For Rod and Lizzie

Scholastic Children's Books
Commonwealth House, 1–19 New Oxford Street,
London WC1A 1NU, UK
a division of Scholastic Ltd
London ~ New York ~ Toronto ~ Sydney ~ Auckland

First published by Scholastic Ltd, 1996

Copyright © David Belbin, 1996

ISBN 0 590 13367 5

Typeset by TW Typesetting, Midsomer Norton, Avon
Printed by Cox & Wyman Ltd, Reading, Berks.

10 9 8 7 6 5 4 3 2

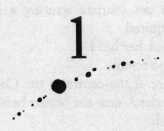

1

"I ought to warn you," Vicki told Andrew as they turned a corner and saw the dark, near derelict house for the first time, "my family are *murder*. It's not too late to turn back."

"Come on," Andrew tried to tease her. "They can't be *that* bad."

Vicki didn't reply. As she slowed the car down, a dark cloud gathered overhead, casting the building before them into an even deeper gloom. It was a huge house, set in the crest between two hills. Dense, deep green ivy covered more than half of its front. There were a few run-down smaller buildings over to one side of it, and what appeared to be a small chapel on the other. Few visitors would expect to find so big a place in the middle of nowhere.

Vicki pulled up outside this vast, grey building.

"Welcome to Hetherington Hall," she said.

"It looks like a stately home," Andrew told her.

"A very small, insignificant one," Vicki assured him.

"Do you get tourists wanting a look inside?" Andrew enquired.

Vicki shook her head.

"We're too remote."

They were at the centre of the Cheviot hills, in Northumberland, near the border between Scotland and England.

"Is it haunted?" Andrew asked, as the big front doors opened.

"Don't be daft," Vicki told him.

A small, moustachioed man in a dark suit came out. He reminded Andrew of an undertaker.

"You must be Miss Victoria." There was a rich Scots lilt to the butler's voice.

"Yes," Vicki said. "And you must be McFadyen. This is my guest, Andrew Wakefield."

The butler met Andrew's eyes with a fake but friendly smile.

"Hallo, sir. Welcome home, miss. How was your journey from West Yorkshire?"

"Slow," Vicki told the butler before he picked up their bags and led the way inside.

"How come he wasn't sure who you were?" Andrew asked, as they climbed the steps into the hall.

"Our old butler died a few weeks ago," Vicki explained. "This is the first time I've met his replacement."

Satisfied, Andrew let himself be led into the deep, dingy hallway. Wide corridors with tiled floors were lined with heavy wooden panels. There was old furniture everywhere, with dark, ornately carved wood. Everything smelt musty. Andrew half expected to see suits of armour and weapons on the walls, but there were only mirrors and dark, dirt-ridden paintings. He wondered why they'd been allowed to get into such a state.

The three of them climbed a winding staircase, then walked along another passage. The butler paused at the end of it before opening the door to a long, narrow room.

"This is where you'll be staying, Mr Wakefield." He put Andrew's rucksack down inside the door.

"The bathroom's down that corridor, off the main landing," the butler pointed out.

"I'll dump my stuff, have a wash, then come back and find you before we meet Mummy," Vicki said.

"Fine," Andrew muttered, as Vicki followed McFadyen to the end of the passage. They went around a corner and out of sight.

Andrew unpacked in a gloomy mood. He hadn't expected to be allowed to stay in the same room as Vicki, but they weren't even going to be in the same part of the house. Not only that, but this room looked like it hadn't been used for at least a century. The smell of damp filled his nostrils. Despite it being sunny and warm outside, the house was chilly. The antique, bronze-coloured radiator in the bedroom gave out no heat whatsoever.

He found the bathroom and was relieved to find that the plumbing worked. The water was hot. There was an old-fashioned, single-bar electric heater on the ceiling. Andrew turned it on with the pull switch by the door and it warmed the room quickly. Feeling more comfortable, Andrew took his time freshening up. He wanted to be at his best when he met Vicki's family.

Back in the bedroom, Andrew hung his one smart jacket in the wardrobe, hoping that the creases would fall out before he needed to wear it again. When he closed the wardrobe door, a large chunk of plaster fell from the ceiling on to the bed. Andrew cursed and looked for a bin to put it in. There wasn't one. He tried to open the window, which looked out on to a steep, Cheviot hill. He meant to throw the plaster out, rather than start on the wrong foot by owning up to the damage, which wasn't his fault. But the window was jammed.

There was a noise on the landing. It sounded like a footstep on creaking floorboards, directly outside the room. Andrew kicked the lump of plaster under the bed, then opened his door. He stepped into the corridor, expecting to see Vicki. Instead, he saw the back of a tall woman with long, dark hair and a full-length dress, walking down the passage, away from him.

Andrew checked his watch. It had been nearly half an hour since McFadyen left him there. Vicki was meant to have come back for him. Where was she?

Andrew walked down the corridor and turned a corner, into darkness. After a moment, his eyes became accustomed to the lack of light caused by the absence of windows. There were rooms to the right, and another, narrow stairway, leading upwards. He continued down the corridor, turned a corner and found a second stairway, going down this time. He took it. The steep stairs twisted and turned. He remembered what Vicki had said about the house, on holiday.

"It's a bit of a ruin. Half of it's not in use. There are doors and stairways which were once important but now don't lead anywhere."

Andrew began to regret going after Vicki. After all, he had no idea where he was, and she would be turning up at his door any moment, wanting to introduce him to her parents.

At the bottom of the stairway, Andrew found himself in a large cellar with a high ceiling and pale stone walls. A passageway trailed off into darkness. There were several doors, all but one of which was closed. Andrew let his curiosity get the better of him. He pulled open the one door which was ajar, and peeked inside.

It was the kitchen. He walked into a well-lit room which smelt of mushy peas and boiled beef. Andrew felt like he'd stepped out of a bad dream into a cosy, picture-postcard past.

"You must be Miss Vicki's friend. Are you lost?"

The woman who'd spoken was small – even smaller than Vicki, who didn't reach Andrew's shoulders – and approaching middle age.

"I was looking for Vicki," Andrew admitted.

"I'm Moira," the woman said. "If you take this stairway over here, you'll find Vicki's room on the second left outside the first door you come to. But don't let her mother or Mr McFadyen catch you using the servants' stairs. They don't like that kind of thing."

When Andrew knocked on Vicki's door, her voice came back quavering and fragile.

"Mummy? I'll only be a moment."

When Vicki opened the door, her hair had been pinned back and she, like the woman he'd seen earlier, was wearing a long dress. Andrew hadn't seen his girlfriend in a dress before. With the change in her hair, it made Vicki seem a different person.

"It's you," she said, relieved, and kissed him. "I'm sorry I've taken so long. I popped down to see Moira in the kitchen."

"I just met her," Andrew said. "She told me

where to find you. You never mentioned that you had servants. Is Moira the cook?"

"Sort of," Vicki said. "Moira's been with the family since she was in her teens. At first, she was the parlour maid. We had lots of servants then. Now she's kind of cook and housekeeper combined. We only have three servants these days. There's a maid who lives out and the butler." She paused, then added, nervously, "I know all this probably seems awfully grand to you, but it's a big house. No one could manage it without staff."

She sounded embarrassed, as well she might. At Bretton, the only sign that Vicki had any money was that she could afford to drive a car – and only a rusty old Mini, at that.

"You could have warned me before we came," Andrew complained.

"I know. But I was glad you wanted to come with me. I thought you might change your mind if I told you too much about … all this. I didn't want to come home alone."

"It's all right." He stroked her bare neck. When her voice went all vulnerable that way, it was hard to deny her anything.

"You're not alone," he whispered. They were about to kiss again when the door behind them opened.

"Victoria!" said a loud, haughty voice. "What *have* you done to your hair?"

Vicki flinched and didn't reply. The voice's owner stepped into the room. She was a tall, wide-shouldered woman, with electric eyes. Andrew had been wondering why Vicki hadn't gone to see her mother as soon as she got home. Now he began to understand. Taking a deep breath, Andrew took a step forward and faced the gorgon.

"I think her hair looks nice long," he said, holding out his hand. "By the way, I'm Andrew."

Nervously, he met her eyes. Vicki's mother frowned for a moment, then, without shaking his hand, looked again at Vicki. Andrew couldn't understand the fuss. He'd encouraged Vicki to let her hair grow over the summer, but, pinned back the way it was, you could hardly tell that it was any longer than it had been when they first met, back in June. The gorgon spoke.

"Make sure you have it cut before your father comes home."

Vicki didn't reply directly.

"Where *is* Daddy?" she asked.

"Abroad. He should get back by the weekend. I phoned to tell him that you were coming, though I didn't mention your ... guest." Now Vicki's mother gave Andrew the smallest possible glance of acknowledgement.

"Why don't you go up and see Cassandra before dinner?" she suggested to Vicki, before departing as abruptly as she'd arrived.

Vicki sat down on her bed, closed her eyes and groaned. Andrew thought of making a comment, but decided against it. Vicki might dislike her mother, but it wasn't done to criticize people's parents. Families were always a sensitive subject.

"Is Cassandra your elder sister?" he asked, when she opened her eyes again. Vicki nodded.

"I saw this woman walking down the passage earlier. She had long dark hair. Would that be her?"

"Yes," Vicki said.

"Should we go and see her?"

"No," Vicki said. "Sandra hates strangers, and I've left you alone long enough. We'll see Sandra if she comes down to dinner." She reached out to him and he sat down next to her on the single bed. They embraced.

"What did you think of my mother?" Vicki asked, when they broke apart.

Andrew tried to think of something tactful to say.

"She's … er, different."

"She's a dragon. It's the only way that she knows how to cope with people. She drives me up the wall."

Andrew said nothing and Vicki sighed.

"Sometimes," she added, "I feel like killing her."

2

A ndrew and Vicki were still in her bedroom an hour later when there was a resonant, clanging sound.

"It's time for dinner," Vicki said. "We'd better go down."

Andrew felt more comfortable walking through the gloomy, draughty house now that he had Vicki's hand in his. They descended the main staircase. As they walked, their reflection appeared in endless antique mirrors: a tall boy in his late teens, with long, curly hair, accompanied by his petite, shy-looking companion.

A large golden gong stood in the hallway, still quietly vibrating. Opposite the bottom of the staircase was the dining-room. If Andrew had been expecting a huge room, capable of hosting a ball, he was disappointed. The dining-room was only the size of a badminton court. There was a grand fireplace opposite the dinner table, but there was no fire in it. The oak table was capable of seating ten or twelve. The room's grey walls were covered in portraits with heavy gilt frames. A few centimetres separated each from the other. Pride of place went to a crystal chandelier which hung over the centre of the table. The room, being in the centre of the house, had no windows. It was very cold.

Only four places were set. Vicki's mother occupied one. A thin boy of eight or nine sat in another.

"Cassandra is eating in her room tonight," Vicki's mother said. "She's disappointed that you haven't been up to see her yet. Paul, this is Andy, Victoria's friend. Andy, my son, Paul." The boy held out his pale, white hand and Andrew shook it. He didn't like being called Andy, but it seemed petty to object.

"Pleased to meet you," he said to Paul.

Vicki's brother was a blue-eyed, blond-fringed boy, with narrow ears and a spaced-out expression.

"Likewise," he replied.

"How's school?" Vicki asked her brother.

"Brilliant. I'm in the hockey team. I can't wait to go back." Paul stopped, apparently aware that his mother might be insulted. If she was at all hurt, she didn't show it.

"His first report was excellent," she boasted to

Vicki. "Much better than yours at his age." As she spoke, Moira brought in the soup and placed it on the table beside Vicki's mother.

"Would you like me to serve, milady?"

"No, no, I'll do it. I wouldn't want you to have an excuse for spoiling the main course."

Moira muttered a patient "Yes, ma'am" as she retreated. Andrew wondered if he was expected to call Vicki's mother "ma'am" or "milady" too. He wondered whether she treated all of the servants as badly as she'd just treated Moira.

Vicki's mother slopped soup into the shallow bowls, complaining about the quality of servants these days as she did so.

"I've tried so many agencies, but you just can't get the staff. Today's Alice's night off, but I asked her to come in because you were coming home, Victoria. And would she? *Terribly* apologetic, of *course*, but she'd made 'other arrangements'."

"How's McFadyen working out?" Vicki asked.

There was a brief, cool pause. Vicki's eyes met her mother's. Andrew gathered that the butler was within earshot.

"Very well," Vicki's mother replied.

The pea and ham soup was delicious. Andrew had a second helping and stopped noticing the cold. As they were finishing, the butler came in.

"Do you require wine with the main course, milady?"

"No wine with dinner until my husband returns," Vicki's mother said. "I won't have anyone disturbing the cellar when he's away, no matter who comes to stay."

The way she said it implied that having guests to dinner was an unusual and disagreeable experience.

"Cellar?" Andrew asked Vicki.

"We have a wine cellar," Vicki explained. "Daddy keeps a lot of rare vintages down there."

"I see."

After Moira had cleared the plates away, there was an awkward gap in the conversation. To fill it, Andrew asked Paul if he was interested in football. Luckily, he was. The new season had just started and the two of them managed to fill the next five minutes discussing various teams' chances of winning the Premier League.

When the meal was over, and Paul was gone, the interrogation began. Vicki's mother swooped like a bird of prey. Andrew half expected to be asked what his "intentions" were towards Vicki. It was nearly that bad. Within five minutes, she'd got more out of Andrew than he had told Vicki in the three months they'd known each other.

"An orphan, you say? You were brought up in an orphanage?"

"No. A boarding school, most of the time."

"Your parents – how did they die?"

"In a car crash."

"And you had no other relatives?"

"Only an aunt. My mother's older sister."

"I see. And this *aunt*, why did she not bring you up?"

"*Mummy!*" Vicki complained. "You shouldn't ask that sort of thing!"

Vicki's mother gave her a glare which made it clear why Vicki didn't stand up to her mother more often.

"It's all right," Andrew said, with a glance at Vicki. "My aunt's much older than my mother ... I mean, than my mother would have been. Her health's not good. She couldn't manage it."

"And what do you live on?"

"There's money – in trust – from my parents' will. The interest paid for my school fees and still gives me some pocket money, but I can't touch the capital until I'm twenty-one."

Vicki gave Andrew a look of surprise. He'd never discussed money with her. But then, she'd never told him that she came from a house like this.

"You must have had a hard life," her mother went on. The words were sympathetic but the tone which Vicki's mother said them in wasn't. She continued the interrogation.

"What course are you on?"

"I'm training to be an art teacher."

"Why?" she said, in a tone which suggested that Andrew's ambitions were hopelessly mediocre.

Before he could reply, Moira came in and cleared the coffee cups away.

"Will there be anything else, milady?"

"No, Moira," her mistress said. "That's all. Good night." Vicki's mother got up to go. She was very much taller than Vicki, Andrew realized, and had a hooked nose which was prominent in profile. She left the room with a regal nod in her daughter's direction. Vicki and Andrew were alone in the draughty dining-room.

"What's all this 'milady' stuff?" Andrew asked. "Is your father *Sir* Hetherington or something?"

Vicki looked embarrassed.

"It's worse than that, I'm afraid. He's a Lord."

"A *Lord*? What does that make you? Lady Victoria?"

Vicki shook her head.

"Mummy's a 'Lady'. I'm not. There are five different types of Lord. Daughters are only called 'Lady' if their father's in the top three: a duke, marquess or earl. With the other two, viscount and baron, sons and daughters are called 'The Honourable'. Daddy's a baron, the lowest kind."

"So he's Baron Hetherington?"

"Only on correspondence and a few official things. Otherwise, he's always referred to as Lord Hetherington."

"And you're the Right Honourable Victoria Hetherington?"

"Just *Honourable*. Not *Right*. I don't use it though. Never have. I'm not even sure I agree with people having titles. Do you?"

"I don't know," Andrew said. "It's not something I've really thought about."

He was still finding the house's atmosphere very oppressive. When he leant forward on the table, something creaked alarmingly. Every time that Andrew touched something, he felt like it was about to break. It would be easier to have this conversation somewhere else – anywhere else.

"I don't suppose there's a pub nearby?" he asked.

"There is one, but it's a twenty mile round journey. You have to be pretty desperate for a pint to go there. We'll go down and see Moira later. She'll find us something to drink."

Vicki stood.

"We'd better go up and meet Sandra. I don't want her to think that we're ignoring her."

Yet isn't she ignoring us, Andrew thought, by not coming down to dinner? But he said nothing. They left the dining-room through a different door and climbed the winding staircase in the centre of the house.

"Sandra has the second floor of the house to herself," Vicki explained. "Has done since I was eight or nine. I used to resent it. I had a room and she had a whole floor. But Sandra's not a person you can envy for long…"

"Why's Sandra like that?" Andrew asked.

"She once had a big disappointment," Vicki explained, in a cautious voice, "and she never got over it."

Before Andrew could ask what the disappointment was, they came out on to the second floor. The landing was even dingier than the floor below, if that was possible. It smelt of mildew.

"Most of this part of the house is closed up," Vicki explained, then pointed at the four doors off the landing. "These used to be guest rooms, but I don't recall us ever having guests in them. The rest of the floor was designed as servants' quarters, but Moira and McFadyen have more comfortable rooms on the first floor." She knocked on one of the doors.

"Sandra, it's me. Sandra?"

There was no reply. But the second floor wasn't silent. Andrew could hear a creaking noise from farther along the landing.

"Do you hear that?" he asked Vicki.

His girlfriend listened.

"Sandra must be doing her exercises," Vicki said. "Please, Andrew, be nice to her. She'll seem strange at first. She's … unusual."

They walked to the end of the landing and turned on to a corridor. This was the front of the house. Through the grimy windows, Andrew could make out a brilliant sunset, shedding its crimson light over the Cheviot hills. The creaking noise grew louder. Vicki knocked on the next door they came to.

"Sandra, it's me."

The creaking stopped. Vicki opened the door. A tall, well-built woman sat on a mat on the floor, wearing a purple leotard. She was using some kind of rowing device and her pale skin glistened with sweat. Her body was that of an athlete. Her long, dark hair must have been like that of Vicki's mother, when she was young. There was a resemblance between mother and daughter. Sandra had a trace of the hooked nose and the aristocratic bearing. But there was a big difference between them, too. Sandra was stunning to look at.

Vicki's sister got up. She gave Vicki a strange, half smile, then she stared at Andrew.

"So," she said. "You found yourself a man."

"This is Andrew."

"A very good-looking one, too."

Andrew mumbled an embarrassed "hallo", and matched Sandra's firm handshake with his own. Sandra addressed her words to both of them, but didn't take her eyes off Andrew.

"As you can see," she said, "I'm half-way through my exercise routine. Why don't I join you when I've finished and showered? Then we can have a chat."

"Great," Vicki said. "We'll be in my room."

"She seems OK," Andrew said, choosing his words

carefully as they walked back downstairs. "Not even unusual."

"That's because we caught her exercising, when she's at her most focused," Vicki said. "She's not always so … relaxed."

"Does she have a job?" Andrew asked.

Vicki shook her head.

"She went to university, but never graduated."

"Why?"

Vicki stopped, faced Andrew, and smiled gently.

"Don't ask me to tell you all our family history at once. Can't you take people as you find them?"

"Of course I can," Andrew said, defensively. "Sandra seems nice."

"She is."

Vicki looked away. During all their conversations over the previous three months, she had barely mentioned Sandra. Andrew was sure that there was a great deal which his girlfriend wasn't telling him. Not for the first time, it occurred to him that he didn't yet know Vicki very well at all.

3

Vicki's room was large but full. There were things everywhere, from furry animals to books and brightly-coloured pottery, making the room a cosy, intimate place. She had a good hi-fi and they listened to music for a while. Then Vicki looked at her watch. It was eight-thirty.

"Moira should have finished her chores for tonight. I'll pop down and visit her, see if she can rustle up a couple of cans of lager for us."

"Fine."

She left Andrew alone in the room. While she was gone, Andrew thought about their relationship. They had been constantly in each other's company for the last three months. So how come now that he was in her home, she felt like a stranger?

His thoughts were interrupted by a knock on the door.

"Come in."

It was Vicki's sister, Sandra. She was dressed casually and had brushed her hair back. Again, Andrew observed that she was a very striking woman.

"Vicki's gone down to see Moira," Andrew explained.

"I'll wait," Sandra said. "If that's all right with you." Sandra's manner was shy, as though she were embarrassed to be alone with Andrew. Yet her eyes examined Andrew so brazenly that he felt he was being appraised, like cattle at an auction.

"How did you and Vicki meet?" Sandra asked.

"We go to the same college," Andrew explained, glad to be on safe ground. "We met back in June. There was an exhibition of Henry Moore sculptures at the West Yorkshire Sculpture Park. It's near the college. I expect you know it?"

Sandra shook her head.

"I don't get out much."

"Anyway, Vicki and I were both looking at one of the pieces and we got talking. One thing led to another. We started going out and, after the exams, went on holiday together. The Greek Islands."

"It sounds idyllic," Sandra said.

"It was."

"And now you're here?"

"Yes."

"And where are you from yourself?"

Andrew took a deep breath, preparing to be asked the questions which he had already covered with Sandra's mother. However, just then, Vicki returned with the drinks.

"Hi, Sandra," she said, with forced cheerfulness.

Vicki had only brought two cans, so Andrew offered to give Sandra his and go for another one. Sandra insisted that she didn't drink. Then the two sisters began talking. At first, Andrew tried to participate, but Vicki and Sandra didn't make much effort to include him. In fact, they behaved as though Andrew wasn't there at all. He watched as the sisters held a detailed, but strained discussion about the family.

Vicki was his girlfriend, but Andrew found it hard to keep his eyes off Sandra. It wasn't that he fancied her, not exactly. Despite her jet black hair and all the exercise she took, the older sister's skin was surprisingly pale, like that of an albino, or a vampire.

Vicki and Sandra talked about their brother, Paul. Sandra felt that, since going away to school, he had changed. He had an unhealthy obsession with what she referred to as "his collection".

"He'll be better once Daddy comes home," Vicki said. "You know how he dotes on Daddy."

"But that's another thing," Sandra said, lowering

her voice, though it was still easy for Andrew to hear every word. "Daddy's up to something."

The conversation continued, but Andrew found it hard to follow. The two sisters weren't speaking in code, not exactly, but all of the conversation's meaning seemed to take place between the lines. It was full of references to events which meant nothing to Andrew, yet everything to them. One thing was clear: both sisters loved their father.

After a while, Andrew had finished his lager.

"Would you like another?" Vicki asked.

"I wouldn't mind," Andrew said, "but I'll go for it myself. Unless there's a bell I can ring for some servant to magically appear with one."

"We do have a bell system," Vicki told him. "But we don't use it in the evening, unless there's an emergency. Both McFadyen and Moira go off duty when they've cleared up after dinner."

"Are you sure that you can find your way to the kitchen?" Sandra asked, with a faint teasing quality to her voice.

"I'll shout if I get lost," Andrew said. "Can I get you something?"

Sandra wanted orange juice, Vicki a coffee. Andrew took the servants' staircase to the kitchen, although he knew he wasn't meant to. He might easily lose his way if he took the other route. Lady Hetherington would be in bed by now, Vicki had said, so she wouldn't object.

The kitchen was no longer brightly lit. A single lamp burned in an alcove near the fridge. Andrew found the orange juice, a jug of milk and the last remaining can of lager. It didn't look like the Hetheringtons were big drinkers. Or eaters: the fridge was practically empty.

Andrew found an electric kettle and put some water on. As the water heated up, he heard a noise, coming from the far end of the kitchen. At first he thought it was a radio. But when the kettle clicked off, he could clearly make out voices. One belonged to Moira:

"You don't know what you're talking about. You've only been here five minutes."

The other was McFadyen's.

"Can't you see what's going on? They're…"

He couldn't make out the rest of the sentence. Moira said something like, "Now that Miss Vicki's home things will be…"

"Never mind Victoria," the butler was saying. "She's not…"

"I've seen this happen before," Moira interrupted, her voice getting louder. "His lordship will work it…" Then there was the sound of a door being shut and the voices became muffled. Andrew put milk into the coffee and walked back up the narrow, winding stairway. Hands full, he pushed open the door which took him on to Vicki's landing.

"Naughty, naughty."

Andrew almost jumped out of his skin. But it was only Sandra.

"You shouldn't use those stairs. They're only for servants. Vicki used to get into an awful lot of trouble going places where she wasn't meant to go when she was younger. I'm surprised she showed you."

"She didn't..." Andrew wouldn't let himself finish the sentence. He didn't want to land Moira in it.

"I've brought you your orange juice," he said, instead.

"Thanks," Sandra said. "I'll take it up to bed with me."

Andrew was carrying Vicki's mug of coffee in his left hand, and had the can of lager and glass of orange juice balanced on top of each other in his right. Sandra carefully removed both items from his right hand, then returned the can, letting her cool fingers linger against his.

"Nice to meet you, Andrew," she said. "Sleep well."

Andrew watched as she drifted down the corridor. He was disturbed that he found her so attractive, even though Vicki was on the other side of the door.

"You're very honoured," his girlfriend said, as he walked in with the drinks. "Sandra likes you. Sandra hardly ever likes anyone. Mind you, she hardly ever meets anyone."

Was now the time to ask Vicki about the secrets in her elder sister's past? Before Andrew could work out how to phrase his question, she was kissing him. Vicki apologized for being distant earlier.

"Coming home always makes me go a bit weird. I was sent off to school when I was Paul's age, and I've always hated having to come home in the holidays. Isn't that weird? For most people, it's the other way round."

"Not me," Andrew said. "I either had to stay in school or visit an aunt who wasn't really interested in me."

"I'm sorry," Vicki said, holding him tight. "You know, we have a lot in common."

"Yes," Andrew said. "I guess we do."

4

Vicki woke Andrew the next morning with breakfast in bed.

"What time is it?" he asked.

It was just after ten, his usual waking time, provided he didn't have a lecture or seminar to go to.

"I always get up earlier at home," Vicki explained. "I forgot to mention – we have breakfast downstairs at eight-thirty. Anyway, look, I got Moira to make you your favourite."

She lifted the cover on his plate to reveal scrambled eggs on wholewheat toast. Andrew was barely awake, and not yet hungry, but he ate it anyway. The eggs were delicious: creamy and almost firm, just the way he liked them. He complimented the cook. While he ate, Vicki talked about all the places they could visit later on.

"You seem in a good mood today," Andrew told her, when he was on to his second cup of tea.

"Daddy rang half an hour ago," Vicki explained. "He'll be home tomorrow morning. I haven't seen him since Easter."

She hadn't seen her mother for the same period of time, Andrew noted, but had spent less than an hour with her since yesterday afternoon.

"So what do you want to do today?" Vicki asked.

"Why don't we start exploring the area straight away, since you say there're so many places to see?"

"Fine," Vicki said. "I'll give you a guided tour. Do you mind if I ask Paul to come along? He could do with the company."

"Not at all," Andrew said. "I'd like to get to know him."

Vicki went for her brother while Andrew dressed. He had a T-shirt around his head when there was a knock on the door. Before he could answer, it opened. The maid came in. She was a slim, pretty girl with a straight blonde bob.

"I'm sorry," she said, backing out of the room. "I came for your breakfast things. I thought…"

"It's all right," Andrew assured her. "Come in. You must be Alice."

The maid nodded.

"I'm Andrew."

"Pleased to meet you," she said, as he fumbled on his socks.

"Have you been with the family long?"

Alice shook her head.

"Since the beginning of summer."

There was no deference or shyness in her voice, Andrew noted. He'd half expected the maid to be a shy, giggly girl, the way they always were in movies. But there was an assurance about Alice. Apart from her uniform, she could have been one of the girls he knew at college.

"Are you local?" Andrew asked, as Alice picked up the tray.

"My family have a farm a few miles away."

"Vicki and I are going for a drive around the area today," Andrew told her, wanting to keep the conversation going. "Is there anywhere that you'd recommend I see?"

"Not today," Alice told him, as she backed out of the room. "It's going to pour with rain in the next half hour. And it'll turn cold. I'd put a sweater on over that T-shirt, if I were you."

Alice was right. By the time Andrew got downstairs, the sky had gone from blue to black. He was waiting for Vicki when Lady Hetherington swept into the hallway.

"I hope you'll be joining us for breakfast in the future," she said, in her irritatingly haughty voice. "We do expect our guests to fit in with the family routine."

"I'm ... sorry," Andrew stuttered. "I didn't know."

Vicki appeared.

"I can't find Paul anywhere," she said to her mother. "Have you seen him?"

"Paul seems to spend most of his time avoiding me this summer," Lady Hetherington moaned. "As you probably gathered last night, he can't wait to go back to school next week. Now you'll excuse me. I have to see McFadyen about the arrangements for your father's return."

She went into one of the rooms off the hallway. Andrew heard a distant bell ringing. As McFadyen scuttled across the hallway, Andrew and Vicki exchanged glances.

"You have to make allowances for Mummy," Vicki said, in a low voice, when the butler was inside the room. "She gets frustrated, being at home all the time. She likes to be in complete control, but there's no one much to be in control of. Daddy's often away. Paul's at school. I'm at college. And Sandra has weeks when she doesn't venture below the second floor."

Andrew nodded understandingly, remembering Vicki's outburst the day before about wanting to kill Lady Hetherington. Probably most people had these contradictory feelings about their parents: sorry for them one minute, wanting to kill them the next. Andrew wouldn't know. Some days, he found it hard even to remember his own parents.

"Uh oh," Vicki said, as thunder sounded from outside. "Maybe that drive isn't such a good idea."

Heavy rain followed a few seconds later. A minute after that, the front door opened and Paul ran in, wearing only shorts and a T-shirt. He was soaked.

"Where've you been?" Vicki asked.

Paul didn't reply.

"Need to go and get changed," he said, brusquely.

"Would you like us to come and play a game with you?" Vicki suggested, generously. "Monopoly, perhaps. Or Cluedo?"

"Not today," Paul told her. "I'm in the middle of mounting the new additions to my butterfly collection." He went upstairs.

"Butterflies?" Andrew asked Vicki.

"The hobby runs in the family. My father. His father. I don't know how far back."

There was a sudden noise behind her and Alice appeared from nowhere. She was carrying a tray with a pot of tea for two on it. Andrew smiled and Vicki spun round. Alice gave her the slightest of nods.

"Oh, Andrew, this is Alice."

"We've met," Andrew said. He smiled at Alice. "You were right about the rain."

Alice smiled back. Earlier her smile had been friendly. Now the look she gave Andrew was unmistakably flirtatious.

"Farmer's daughter," Alice said, before taking the tray into the room where Lady Hetherington was meeting with McFadyen.

"We should never have taken her on," Vicki said, even though the door was still half open. There was jealousy in her voice.

"Why?" Andrew asked.

Vicki didn't reply. Had she caught him looking admiringly at the maid? Most people would think that Alice was prettier than she was. Did Vicki think that Andrew fancied Alice? Was she that insecure? As far as Andrew knew, he was her first boyfriend.

Or maybe it was a class thing. Maybe, Andrew realized, it wasn't done for him to chat freely with the servants. But Vicki was on close terms with Moira, wasn't she? He might be a guest in Vicki's home, but that didn't mean that he had to adopt all the double standards of the English upper classes.

The rain didn't let up all day. Andrew's girlfriend stayed in a frosty mood, without explaining the reason why. Andrew wanted to look around the Hall, but Vicki wasn't keen to show him.

"Not while Mummy's home," she said. "Mummy doesn't like people nosing around. Daddy once suggested opening the place to the public, just for a few days a year. Mummy freaked out."

"But I'm not the public. I'm your boyfriend."

"Mummy's always hated my friends coming to visit. She did everything she could to discourage it."

"So how come she's let me stay now?" Andrew asked.

"I didn't give her a choice," Vicki explained. "I didn't ask her whether you could come. I simply wrote a letter home saying that I was bringing you. After all," she added, reaching forward and hugging him, "we've just spent the entire summer together. It's about time you met my family. I'm sure that you and Daddy will get on famously."

"Yes," said Andrew. "I'm sure we will."

Dinner was an even glummer affair than the night before. Andrew asked Lady Hetherington a bland question about what the neighbours were like.

"There are no *families* around here," Lady Hetherington complained. "No one of note. For years, I tried to persuade Victoria's father to build a place in Hexham – he is Lord Hetherington of Hexham, you know – but he wouldn't hear of it. He prefers to be here, in the wilderness."

But he isn't here at the moment, Andrew thought.

Alice began to serve the main course, a roast dinner. Lady Hetherington put her finger to the gravy boat.

"This gravy is barely lukewarm," she complained. "Take it down to the kitchen and have Moira heat it properly."

Alice gave a bland apology and left the room. Steam rose from the other dishes. Alice took her time. Andrew watched as the rest of the food went cold.

After dinner, Paul hurried upstairs to continue

work on his collection. He said that he wanted his new butterflies mounted in time to show to Lord Hetherington on his return the next day. Lady Hetherington rang the bell for Alice to clear the coffee cups.

"And run me a bath before you go home," she ordered the maid. "It's been a very wearing day."

As far as Andrew could tell, Vicki's mother had done no work of any kind whatsoever.

"Remember," she said to Andrew before going upstairs. "Breakfast is at eight-thirty sharp."

"Want to watch some telly?" Vicki asked, when her mother was gone.

"Sounds like a good idea to me."

"I'll just pop upstairs and see how Sandra is. God knows when she ever eats. Do you mind if I try to persuade her to join us?"

"No. Fine."

While Vicki was gone, Andrew decided to go upstairs and put on a warmer sweater. The Hall was even colder at night, but the radiators still weren't on. He took the main stairway. The sound of running water could be heard through the wooden panels on the walls. Then it stopped. Andrew nearly bumped into Alice on the landing.

"Does this house ever get warm?" he asked her.

"I thought you'd got Miss Victoria to keep you warm," Alice teased. "Isn't she doing a good enough job?"

Andrew blushed. He had been around enough girls to know when someone fancied him. Until this moment, he hadn't really thought of the maid in a sexual way. But, now, he and Alice stood next to each other on the landing, close enough to feel the heat from each other's bodies. He wanted to touch her. There were also questions which Andrew wanted to ask, but he didn't know the right way to begin. Then there was the sound of a car hooting outside.

"That'll be my father, come to pick me up," Alice told him.

"I'll see you again," Andrew said, trying to keep his voice warm, but not too warm. Alice didn't reply. She skipped down the stairs, as though she was ecstatically happy to be getting out of Hetherington Hall.

"This is the TV room," Vicki told Andrew, a few minutes later. "Sandra was exercising, but she said that she might come down to join us, later."

At last, Andrew felt like he was back at the turn of the twenty-first century, not the twentieth. The room had a wide-screen TV with surround sound speakers, a stereo video and a satellite decoder. There were two comfy-looking sofas. There was even a small gas fire, which Andrew switched on.

"Daddy likes his comforts," Vicki said. "What do you want to watch?"

"Why don't we see what's on?" Andrew suggested.

Vicki pressed a button on the TV and immediately, before the picture appeared, there was a loud, ear-piercing scream which seemed to come from the back of the room.

"Amazing sound," Andrew said.

"That wasn't the TV!" Vicki shouted, rushing to the door. "That was my mother!"

5

The bathroom was in the middle of the second floor, close to the landing. Vicki and Andrew got to the door just as Sandra came hurtling down the stairs. McFadyen almost collided with Vicki's sister as he reached the landing. Moira followed behind. All five of them converged on the bathroom door, which was locked.

"Mummy!" Vicki called, shaking the door handle. "Mummy, are you all right?"

No answer.

"Stand aside," McFadyen said. He barged the door twice with his shoulder, but it didn't budge.

"Help me," he asked, and Andrew stepped forward. Between them, they managed to kick the door in.

"Oh, God!"

The voice was McFadyen's. Sandra followed him into the bathroom, and promptly fainted. As the butler leant down to help Sandra up, Andrew saw what they had seen. Lady Hetherington lay in the bath. The infra-red heater fitting floated beside her body, sizzling. Wires trailed from the ceiling. Andrew reached for the heater's pull switch and turned the lethal contraption off. It was too late though. Lady Hetherington's body had turned a horrible colour.

She was dead.

Vicki finally got in, saw what Andrew had seen, and screamed. He guided her back on to the landing and held her. On the floor, Sandra was coming round.

"Is she? Is she?"

"I'm afraid so," McFadyen said.

Moira was the last into the bathroom. She came out, shaking her head, then shut the door behind her.

"I always said those electric heaters on the ceiling were dangerous," she said to McFadyen. "Especially in an old house like this. Will I call for an ambulance?"

"Yes," the butler told her. "Better call the police, too. If we don't, the ambulance people will."

The housekeeper left. Sandra and Vicki were still sitting next to each other on the floor, in tears.

Andrew sat down and held Vicki, who was

shaking. When Moira returned from calling the emergency services, he asked the housekeeper if she'd make some hot, sweet tea.

"I was about to suggest the same thing," Moira said.

A few minutes later, they were drinking tea in the dining-room, speechless from the shock. It was only when they were on their second cup that Vicki thought of something they'd all forgotten.

"Little Paul!" she said. "Where is he? Suppose he stumbles into the bathroom and finds Mummy like, like … that?"

"I'll find him," McFadyen said.

"No," Vicki said. "I'd better do it."

"Are you sure you're all right to?" Andrew asked her.

"I will be if you come with me," she said. "I know where he is."

Andrew followed willingly as Vicki climbed two flights of stairs.

"He uses the attic because it's a good place to dry out his butterflies before he preserves them," she told Andrew, as they walked across the dusty second storey of the building. The floorboards creaked and spiders' webs criss-crossed the ceiling. Andrew could almost believe that the webs were holding the ceiling up.

The attic was reached from a black, wrought-iron

spiral staircase at the back of the second floor. Andrew's head brushed more cobwebs as they made their way up to the dark, dusty attic. Andrew found the place creepy and threatening. Whatever Vicki said, he thought that an attic was an odd place for a young boy to spend a lot of his time. Vicki gripped his hand as they clambered into it.

"This is going to be difficult," she said. "Help me."

"Paul?" Andrew called. He could make out a light off to their right, beneath the high rafters.

"Who's there?" Paul replied, nervously. "What do you want?"

"It's Andrew and Vicki," Vicki called. "We need to talk to you."

"Can't it wait?" Paul asked, impatiently. "I'm in the middle of something."

Andrew approached Paul, surprised to find him so assertive. There was a horrible smell coming from his direction. Andrew thought that he knew what it was: formaldehyde, the chemical used for preserving dead bodies. Paul was standing over a huge sink, surrounded by chemicals. Dozens of butterflies were laid out on paper beside it. A large, old-fashioned metal lamp was clamped to the sink, illuminating the jars of chemicals which surrounded Paul.

"Aren't some of those chemicals rather dangerous?" Andrew asked.

"Daddy showed me how to use them."

Andrew trod cautiously on the shadowy floor, wary of holes in the boards. Then he nearly tripped on an electric wire as he got nearer to the boy. Beside Paul, pale butterflies were laid out on brown parcel paper.

"How do you catch them?" Andrew asked Paul. "With a net?"

Paul gave him a condescending nod.

"And then?"

Paul frowned.

"Then I kill them, of course."

"Of course."

Vicki leant forward and put a hand on Paul's shoulder.

"Paul, can you come downstairs with us? We've got something to tell you."

"I can't leave this. Tell me up here."

"This isn't the right place," Andrew tried to explain. "I think you'll want to be downstairs."

"What is it?" Paul said, impatiently. "Are you two getting married? Congratulations and everything, but I really don't see…"

"It's nothing like that," Vicki replied, abruptly. Then she put on a pleading voice which Andrew hadn't heard her use before. "Please come downstairs with us, Paul. You can come back to this later."

Paul continued mixing chemicals.

"Give me two minutes," he said. "You can wait for me on the landing."

Andrew was glad to get out of the dusty attic, with its threatening shadows.

"How does Paul stand it up there?" he asked Vicki. "At his age, it would have given me nightmares."

"He's been going up there with Daddy since he was five," Vicki explained. "Daddy can't manage the stairs himself any more. He wanted Paul to carry on the work. But since he went away to school, he's had a lot to do in the holidays. His being up there might seem odd to us, but it's normal to Paul, I guess. I wish he'd hurry up."

Her brother took nearly ten minutes to come down. Andrew began to worry that the police would show up before he appeared. While they waited, Vicki brushed the cobwebs from his hair. For someone whose mother had just died in a terrible accident, she was remarkably calm. Maybe, Andrew thought, it was because she had to be responsible for Paul. Any other explanation was too cruel to countenance.

Eventually, the boy came out on to the landing, entering the dank air like an astronaut reluctantly returning to Earth.

"Well?" he said. "What is it?"

"It's Mummy," Vicki told him, in a quiet voice. "She's had an accident."

"What kind of accident?"

"A very bad one."

Paul looked from Vicki to Andrew and back

again. A boy his age should be able to understand death, Andrew thought, especially one who caught butterflies. But Vicki couldn't bring herself to say the words.

"Your mother had an accident in the bath," Andrew told Paul in his gentlest voice. "I'm afraid that she's dead."

Paul's reaction wasn't one of pain or sorrow. In fact, for a moment, Andrew thought he saw the hint of a smile crossing the boy's lips. But his expression remained as distant as ever.

"I'm sorry to hear that," he said. "Can I go back to mounting my butterflies now?"

Vicki burst into tears. Andrew didn't know what to say. Paul stared at them, politely waiting for permission.

"Can I go?" he repeated.

"Go," Andrew told him. The boy scurried off. Vicki wept on to Andrew's shoulder.

"He's too young to really understand," he tried to explain. "The grief'll hit him later, the way it's hitting you now."

"Is this grief?" Vicki asked. "I don't know what it is. I'm not crying for her, I'm crying for me. Paul's reaction was more honest than mine. I'm crying because she never loved me, and I never loved her. Do you understand?"

Andrew wasn't sure that he did, but couldn't say that.

"I think so."

"Do you?" Vicki demanded, her voice becoming harder. "I'm crying because I'm glad that she's dead."

The emergency services took a long time coming. After a while, everyone congregated in the sitting-room, a vast room at the front of the house where Lady Hetherington had had her conference with McFadyen earlier in the day.

The sitting-room contained several ancient sofas, upholstered in velvet and heavily padded. There was also a chaise longue and numerous armchairs. Andrew thought it was the pleasantest room in the Hall. There was a feeling of space in it. The cream walls were recently painted, and less crowded with pictures than elsewhere in Hetherington Hall. The ornate plasterwork was in relatively good condition. A real fire burnt in the hearth so that, despite the high ceiling, it was warm. At any other time, it would have been a cheerful room.

"They've probably lost their way," Moira said. "It's easily done, after dark."

Andrew went to the window. Since this was the ground floor, the windows were clean on the inside as well as out, but he could make out no headlights in the distance.

"I'll ring them again," McFadyen said, leaving the room.

Everyone else sat in silence. Moira had her arms around Paul, who looked vulnerable but bored. Sandra wore a dress now – though not the one Andrew had seen her in the day before. It was a summer dress, but the style was very old-fashioned. It didn't fit her well either, being far too tight around the shoulders and upper arms. She must have bought it before she began her body-building exercises.

Andrew felt uneasy. He didn't belong with the Hetheringtons at a time like this. What made everything even more awkward was the way none of them seemed very upset by Lady Hetherington's death.

"They should be here any minute," McFadyen said as he came back into the room. Andrew got up.

"I think I'll take a look from an upstairs window, see if I can see them coming."

No one argued, so Andrew went up the side staircase and found his way to one of the front windows on the first floor. It was hard to see much beyond the shape of the hills in the night sky. Still, Andrew didn't relish rejoining the others in the sitting-room for a while, so he went up to the next floor. There were no lights to be seen from this height, either, but he waited there anyway.

Lady Hetherington's death bothered Andrew. He'd never seen death at close hand before, but that wasn't the reason. Everyone assumed that what happened was an accident. It seemed an unlikely one to him. What made the heater fall down? He wanted to take a look, before the police got there and – presumably – sealed the room off. How did you get to the bathroom from here? Andrew went back towards the main staircase, hoping that he wouldn't take a wrong turn. He stopped outside a room which he figured should be above the bathroom, and opened the door.

The room turned out to be Sandra's exercise room. Andrew had an idea. He turned the light on. If he was right, beneath these bare floorboards must be the hole in the ceiling where the wall heater had fallen. He might be able to work out what caused the accident to happen.

The floorboards were long and went from one end of the big room to the other. There was no way of lifting them. Luckily, however, some of them were cut into sections. He lifted one. Only darkness below. He lifted another. There was a chink of light to one side. Had the bathroom light been left on? Andrew couldn't remember anyone turning it off. If it was the bathroom beneath, then he only had to go a little to one side. Andrew moved Sandra's rowing machine and lifted the mat. Sure enough, sections of board had been cut, maybe to install the heater, years ago. He removed one of the sections.

Beneath the beams, Andrew could see where the plaster had given way. The wires were clipped along the beams, but the last two clips were missing. Enough wire had been freed for the heater to reach the bath and remain live. It was possible to see where the heater had been mounted, to one side of the bath. But the electric wires came in over the bath. When the heater came loose and fell, the pressure from the wires would cause it to swing in, on to and into the bath.

The cause of the accident was obvious. Moisture from the bathroom had weakened the plaster on the ceiling, causing it to crumble. At the same time, vibrations from the rowing machine above must have weakened the screws which attached the heater to a joist in the ceiling. The only mystery was where the clips which attached the wires to the beams had gone. Andrew guessed that pressure from the falling heater had caused them to spring out. They must be on the bathroom floor. He had no intention of going into the bathroom to make sure. Andrew already knew all he wanted to know. It *was* an accident – an easily preventable one, but an accident nevertheless.

He returned the mat and the rowing machine, then went back to the window at the front of the house. In the distance, he could make out small pin-pricks of light, moving. Help was on its way.

6

The doctor quickly pronounced Lady Hetherington dead and an ambulance took her body away. The police stayed longer. The investigating officer, Detective Sergeant Sinclair, spoke to everyone. He asked Andrew a few cursory questions, then, finally, addressed Sandra, as she was the senior member of the family present.

"There'll have to be an inquest, but the result is a foregone conclusion: accidental death."

"What caused the accident?" Moira asked.

"The heater shouldn't have been placed so close to the bath in the first place," the sergeant told her. "I've examined the ceiling. The plaster was weak because of the moisture, but the actual cause of the accident was that the heater had worked itself loose over the years. Does anyone know when it was installed?"

"It was here when I arrived, twenty years ago," Moira said.

"Has the house been rewired, or have there been safety checks in that time?"

"Not to my knowledge," McFadyen told him, "but I've only been with the family for a few months. I could check the house records."

"Who is responsible for maintenance?"

McFadyen looked embarrassed.

"There used to be a handyman," Moira said. "But that position has been vacant for some time."

McFadyen coughed.

"Technically, it's my responsibility. When things about the house break, I get them repaired. There was, as far as I know, no indication that the heater was about to fall. Otherwise... The servants, naturally, use a different bathroom."

"Naturally," the sergeant agreed, in a sardonic tone. "I won't trouble you any further."

He turned to face the others.

"Again, my commiserations for your loss. A police photographer will be along in the morning. Until then, please stay out of the bathroom."

It was nearly ten when the police left. Vicki tried to ring her father in South Africa, but he was already on the plane home. Vicki left a message at the

Gatwick Hotel where he usually stayed after a long flight.

"I think," McFadyen said, "that this is an appropriate time for us to retire."

The butler left. Moira followed him, after some whispered words of sympathy to Vicki and Paul. She didn't, Andrew noticed, say anything to Sandra. He went over to Vicki, thinking that there was now nothing to stop them spending the night together. He was wrong.

"Would you share my room?" Sandra asked Vicki. "I don't want to be alone tonight."

"Of course," Vicki said. "Paul, would you like Andrew to sleep in your room?"

"I'm OK," Paul said.

"I think it would be better if he did," Sandra said. "You know how you wake in the night sometimes, Paul."

Paul looked embarrassed and annoyed in equal measures, but agreed to let Andrew share his room. Vicki gave her boyfriend a small squeeze good night, then she was gone.

Paul's room seemed to belong to another world. One wall was covered with football posters, the others with pictures of wildlife, predominantly butterflies. There were plenty of toys and comic books. It was a comfortable, warm place. The same couldn't be said for the pre-war camp bed which

Sandra gave Andrew to sleep on. Parts of it dug into his back so sharply that he ended up folding away the bed and sleeping on the floor.

Andrew tried to make more light conversation with Paul, but the boy wouldn't talk. Soon, he seemed to be asleep. Andrew was exhausted, but couldn't get off himself. The events of the day kept running through his mind. He wondered if the Detective Sergeant had gone up and checked out the exercise room. Had the police realized that the rowing machine was directly above the bath? Andrew decided that they probably had. They wouldn't mention it to the Hetheringtons because it might upset Sandra when she realized that she was partly responsible for the accident.

Andrew finally started drifting off to sleep at around midnight. He wasn't, however, completely under when a noise disturbed him. At first, he thought it came from someone moving about above his head. But that couldn't be. The rooms above were disused servants' quarters. Then the door creaked open.

Andrew was sleeping on the floor at the foot of Paul's bed and couldn't see very well. He wriggled his head around the bed, in case it was Vicki and she needed him. But it wasn't. The shadow in the doorway was taller: Sandra. She closed the door behind her, then leant down over Paul's bed.

"Are you all right?" she said in a low voice.

Andrew was about to say something when, to his surprise, Paul replied immediately.

"I'm fine. Andrew's sleeping in my room tonight," he whispered. "Don't wake him up."

"OK. I was worried about you. Sleep well. One day, all of this will seem like a bad dream."

She kissed him on the forehead and left. Andrew tried to get back to sleep, but was confused by this nocturnal visit. On the one hand, he found it touching that Sandra was so caring about her brother. But it was odd that she seemed to have forgotten that Andrew was in Paul's room. Unless…

What if Sandra hadn't expected Paul to be awake, but had been addressing her question to Andrew? What if…? But no, that was ridiculous. Andrew was years younger than Sandra, and he was Vicki's boyfriend. She wouldn't try to … would she?

When Andrew woke in the morning, Paul was already gone. It was twenty to nine. Andrew dressed in the clothes he'd worn the night before and went looking for a bathroom. There must be at least one other bathroom on this floor. But if there was, he couldn't find it. Andrew couldn't even find his own room, where the rest of his clothes were. There would be a bathroom, he guessed, on Sandra's floor, but that was the last place he wanted to go that morning.

On the ground floor, Andrew found a toilet, and

washed his face in the hand basin outside it. Then he went to the gloomy dining-room. It was empty and cold. No one had eaten there that morning. Andrew was about to leave the room to continue looking for Vicki, when he noticed a bell pull. He couldn't resist the temptation, and tugged it. There was no sound, so he tugged it again. Probably broken for decades, he decided.

Suddenly, out of nowhere, McFadyen appeared.

"You rang, Mr Andrew?"

It took Andrew a moment or two to recover his composure.

"I'm sorry, yes. Where is everyone? I mean, where do I get a breakfast?"

"Miss Victoria is in the breakfast room with Miss Cassandra. I'll take you there."

The breakfast room was on the other side of the hall from the dining-room. It had its own dumb waiter, through which food was brought up from the kitchen in the basement. Sandra was already gone. Vicki had almost cleared her plate.

"Andrew! There's plenty of kedgeree left in the dish. Shall I send it down to be heated up? Or would you like something different?"

He inspected the lukewarm fish and rice dish. It smelt delicious.

"This'll be fine as it is," he said. "Is there any tea?"

Vicki asked McFadyen to make a fresh pot.

"How did you sleep?" she asked Andrew.

"Fine," he lied.

"I didn't want to disturb you. Is Paul still in bed, too?"

"No," Andrew told her. "He was gone when I got up. Hasn't he been down for breakfast?"

Vicki shook her head.

"He's behaving very strangely at the moment."

"Surely, his mum dying…"

"I know, but before that – last night at dinner – and then, when we went up to see him in the attic, how did he seem to you?"

"Odd," Andrew admitted. "Spaced out, like he was short on sleep, or ill. But I assumed that he was always that way."

"No," Vicki said. "He used to be a normal, healthy, cheerful, affectionate boy. He's changed."

"Perhaps it's to do with being away at school," Andrew said, remembering Vicki's discussion with Sandra two nights before. "We covered it in my first year B.Ed. lectures. Kids often cope with separation from their parents by distancing themselves. That way, they don't have to acknowledge how much they're hurt by being sent away."

"Maybe that's it," Vicki said, as Andrew began to eat his kedgeree. "Adjusting to boarding school is difficult at first. Though I think Mummy and Daddy were right to send us all there. It's so isolated here. You can't learn to make friends unless you mix with other people your own age."

"I guess not."

Alice brought in a fresh pot of tea. She was followed by McFadyen.

"The police photographers have arrived," he said. "I can't find Miss Cassandra. Do you want to deal with them, Miss Victoria?"

"I'll do it," Vicki said, and left the room with the butler.

Andrew was glad to find himself left alone with Alice. The maid seemed to be lingering in the breakfast room. As she brushed crumbs from the table, her body rubbed briefly against his. Andrew pretended not to notice, but began a conversation.

"You must have been shocked when you came in this morning."

"I think her ladyship was the one who got the shock," Alice replied, curtly, as she collected more of the breakfast dishes.

"Sorry," Andrew told her. "Accidental pun."

"Some families have more accidents than others," Alice said, with a mysterious smile. He wanted to keep talking to her, but she walked out of the room before he could think of a reply. He abandoned his kedgeree and went up to the first-floor landing. The police were packing away.

"You can have the ceiling fixed now," the sergeant was saying.

"McFadyen will organize it," Vicki told him. "Though, personally, I don't think I'll ever be able to use this room again."

Andrew looked into the bathroom. The water had been drained from the bath, and the wall heater removed. There was still some plaster on the floor, but nothing to suggest that a tragedy had occurred there.

"Have you taken anything away?" he asked the sergeant.

"Only the wall heater. A report will have to be done on it."

Andrew thought of mentioning the clips which were missing, the ones which should have held the electric wires to the joist. If they had held, the accident needn't have happened. But if he remarked their absence, it would be obvious he'd been in Sandra's room, looking for clues. Andrew didn't want to draw attention to his own morbid curiosity.

He and Vicki saw the police officers to the door. As their car pulled away, another came up the driveway. McFadyen hurried out to the front doors and opened them fully as a Bentley parked in the drive. A portly man in late middle age got out of the car.

"At last," Vicki said, before she ran over to greet him. "It's my father."

7

"Need a stiff drink," Vicki's father said, after greeting his younger daughter and butler. McFadyen brought him a tumbler containing two inches of pale whisky, which the Baron downed in two gulps. The butler stood to attention while Vicki and her father sat in the easy chairs of the drawing-room. Andrew stood uneasily at their side.

"Another," Lord Hetherington commanded.

McFadyen returned with the bottle, a twenty-seven-year-old single malt. It was only as he sipped this second drink that his lordship seemed to notice Andrew.

"Who the hell are you?" he asked. "New groundsman? I don't remember telling McFadyen to take on another servant."

"This is Andrew," Vicki told her father. "He's my boyfriend." Lord Hetherington blinked twice, then held out his hand.

"Any friend of Vicki's is a friend of mine."

"I'm sorry we aren't meeting under happier circumstances," Andrew told him, not sure whether he ought to be adding "m'lord" to the end of each sentence. Lord Hetherington gave him an abrupt nod of acknowledgement then proffered the whisky bottle.

"Drink?"

"A bit early in the day for me."

"What's your name again? Where are your family from?"

Andrew answered the first question quickly, ducking the second.

"Wakefield. Andrew Wakefield."

"Wakefield. That's where Vicki's at college. Local boy, eh?"

"I'm at the college, too. Training to be an art teacher."

This seemed to satisfy Lord Hetherington's curiosity for the moment.

"Where's my Paul?"

"He had breakfast early," Vicki told her father. "He's probably in the attic, with his butterflies. Shall I get him?"

"No, no. Let him keep at it. And Sandra?"

"Gone for a walk, I think."

"Is she…?"

There was some kind of secret communication passing between father and daughter, Andrew saw. Vicki replied in a tone which made it sound like she was speaking of an invalid, or a very small child.

"Better than normal, I'd say. I think with Andrew here, and the police, she's been on her best behaviour."

"Good, good."

His drink finished, Lord Hetherington got up from his easy chair. He showed no sign of the alcohol having affected him.

"Family meeting later tonight. A lot to discuss. Till then, arrangements to be made. I'll be in my study. McFadyen, make sure Paul comes to see me when he emerges, won't you?"

"Yes, m'lord."

He fondly kissed Vicki on the forehead.

"Good to have you home, my dear."

"Good to have *you* home."

Vicki and Andrew were alone again.

"How are you?" he asked, coming over to sit on the arm of her chair.

"I'm fine. I'm glad Daddy's back. He spends a lot of time away. I thought he might be gone for days."

"What does he do?" Andrew wanted to know.

"He has … business interests. I think part of the reason he stays away so much is that he and Mummy don't … didn't get on. Not for a long time.

That's also one reason why she was … the way she was."

Andrew waited to see if Vicki added anything to this. She got up.

"Why don't we go for a walk?" Vicki suggested. "There are all those wonderful walks I told you about yesterday. And I need to get outside, clear my head."

"Good idea," Andrew agreed enthusiastically.

The sky was a brilliant blue. It was the first week of September, but felt more like high summer. The landscape was a blizzard of purples, browns and different shades of green.

"You must get a lot of walkers around here," Andrew commented.

"Surprisingly few," Vicki told him. "You see, there's so much beautiful countryside here and in Scotland, but the population's tiny. Also, we're right in the middle of the Cheviots. Unless you know your way around, there's no way you can drive somewhere and do a short, scenic, circular walk. So only the most intrepid hikers tend to make it this far in."

"You're very lucky to have so much beauty to yourselves."

They held hands and followed a sheep path along the edge of a tree-lined hill. A little later, they came to a small pool filled with water lilies and sat by it. On the banks of the pool were some wooden huts, partly concealed by the long grass and bracken which had begun to turn brown.

"What are they?" Andrew asked Vicki.

"Can't you tell?"

He examined one. The huts had no roof and were open on one side. Each had a wooden seat built into it. Andrew was mystified until he got in and spotted some red plastic casings, littering the ground.

"Shooting."

"Yes. They hide themselves in there, then pop up and shoot when the birds fly overhead. Grouse mostly, and pheasants. Daddy used to have big parties over every summer, but lately his health hasn't been so good. They're hardly used now."

They stood there, looking at the rolling hills, purple with heather. This must be paradise, Andrew thought to himself. For a few moments, he forgot Lady Hetherington's death. He put aside his attraction to Alice, and stopped thinking about the maid's enigmatic words that morning. Instead, Andrew looked at Vicki and she looked at him.

"This place is wonderful," he said. "I love it."

"I knew you would," she said, hugging him. "I knew it."

As they walked back to the Hall, dark clouds began to sail in from the south. Their gentle walk became a mad dash to avoid the rain.

8

L ord Hetherington met Andrew and Vicki at the front door.

"Did you see Sandra on your walk?" he asked.

"No," Vicki told him.

Andrew hadn't given Vicki's sister a moment's thought while they were out.

"Has Paul come down?" Vicki asked.

"Yes. We've been looking at his butterflies. How do you think he's taken it?"

"I'm not sure," Vicki said. "He's not really himself."

Her father agreed.

"I shouldn't have stayed away so long. Couldn't be helped, but there it is."

Vicki smiled sympathetically.

"No one's blaming you, Daddy."

"Thing is, I am to blame in a way. If the house had been properly maintained ... place should have been rewired back in the seventies ... sixties even ... always putting things off, your grandfather was. And I'm the same. Can't be helped. She's gone now. Maybe it's for the best. She had a miserable life, poor old bird."

Vicki didn't reply. A telephone rang nearby. Andrew looked around and saw a black Bakelite phone in a nest under the stairwell.

"Isn't one of you going to answer that?" he asked.

Lord Hetherington looked at Andrew as though he'd made an impertinent remark.

"It's normally the butler's job," Vicki explained.

"McFadyen's driven to Kelso to buy some supplies," Lord Hetherington said, as the phone continued ringing.

"Why don't I answer it?" Andrew suggested. Un-answered telephones got on his nerves almost as much as unnecessary etiquette. He picked up the phone before Vicki or her father could reply.

"Hetherington Hall," he said, into the crackly mouthpiece.

"May I speak to Lord Hetherington?" a female, professional-sounding voice asked.

"Who shall I say is calling?"

"My name's Mary Rutherford, Doctor Mary Rutherford."

Andrew covered the mouthpiece. "A Doctor Mary Rutherford for you," he said to his lordship.

"Ask her what she wants."

"Could I ask you what the call's about, Doctor?"

"No. I do need to speak to Lord Hetherington in person."

Andrew covered the mouthpiece again and passed this information on. Reluctantly, Lord Hetherington went to the phone.

"Hallo, hallo? What can I do for you, Doctor? Hallo? Anyone there? Hallo?" He put the phone down. "Woman must have hung up."

Andrew picked up the phone again and listened. There was no dialling tone.

"It's completely dead."

"Nuisance," Lord Hetherington complained. "McFadyen can sort it out later. What are you two up to now? Got any plans?"

"Nothing much," Vicki said.

"No studying to do?"

Andrew hadn't brought a single book with him, but Vicki made a pretence of having some work which needed doing.

"Then go and do it, child. Why don't I show you the library, my boy? Are you interested in our family's history?"

"Yes. Of course I am."

"Daddy!" Vicki complained. "You'll bore Andrew senseless."

"Nonsense. You go and get your work done. I'll return Andrew in time for afternoon tea."

They walked across the house. Andrew liked Lord Hetherington more than he had expected to. He seemed to be old-fashioned but, etiquette aside, not stuffy or stuck up. As they walked, he and the old man talked first about South Africa, then about Vicki.

"She seems very happy, Andrew. I think I must have you to thank for that."

Andrew stuttered something in reply. Talk of happiness the day after Lady Hetherington's death seemed misplaced, somehow.

The library was a grand, dark room at the back of the house. It was full of bookcases with glass doors. Inside them were endless hardbacked books, the majority bound in leather. There were some more modern books: a complete *Oxford English Dictionary* and the current volume of *Debrett's Peerage*, but no paperbacks whatsoever. The majority of the volumes seemed to be chronicles of Northumberland. Others were bound scrapbooks, of a sort. They were called "house" books, and detailed visitors, expenses, births, deaths, employment of servants and so on, handwritten by the Lord Hetherington of the time.

The present Lord Hetherington showed these to Andrew. Some of the photographs were of his ancestors with members of the royal family and other famous people. But none were recent. Andrew got the impression that the family no longer moved in those circles.

He was hoping to see some early pictures of Vicki, but these weren't on offer. The nearest he got was the family's entry in *Debrett's*. His host was, the book confirmed, Lord Hetherington of Hexham – Hexham being a market town south of the Cheviots. He was a "baron by writ" whose family was ennobled in the Middle Ages. The family built Hetherington Hall in the second half of the nineteenth century.

"Do you have any pictures of Vicki when she was young?" Andrew asked, as her father put down the book covering the years between the First and Second World Wars.

Before he could answer, Lord Hetherington had a coughing fit. Andrew stood back, waiting for it to end. The fit went on and on, alarming him. Lord Hetherington was turning blue in the face.

What to do? Andrew knew next to nothing about first aid. The only thing he could think to do was to run out of the library in search of help. Then, in a corner of the room, he noticed the bell pull and hurried to it. Within moments of his call, McFadyen was in the room with them. His lordship was sitting on the floor, coughing blood.

"He's been like this for a couple of minutes. Can

you get him some water, quickly?" Andrew pleaded.

The butler ignored him. He darted forward, reached into one of Lord Hetherington's pockets and produced a small blue pill. Then he performed a delicate manoeuvre which involved tilting his lordship's head back and inserting the pill under his tongue. Lord Hetherington stopped coughing.

McFadyen went to one of the bookcases, which, when pulled out, became a drinks cabinet. There was a decanter filled with water. McFadyen poured some of it into a heavy crystal glass and passed it to Lord Hetherington. When Vicki's father failed to take the glass McFadyen tipped the water into his mouth, a little at a time.

"His lordship needs to rest," McFadyen told Andrew when he'd finished. "Alice will be serving afternoon tea in the sitting-room in a few minutes. You can join Miss Victoria there."

Andrew did as he was told. Vicki was waiting for him on one of the big sofas.

"I hope Daddy hasn't been boring you to death," she said.

"It was quite … interesting," Andrew replied. "But your father had a bit of a funny turn."

He told her about the coughing fit and McFadyen administering the pill. Before he could finish, Vicki ran off to see her father.

"Daddy has a heart condition," Vicki explained, when she returned, a few minutes later. "And a bad chest. He probably talked too much when he was with you. Don't worry. The doctors say that he's good for years and years yet if he takes it easy. He'll join us when he's had a little rest."

She poured some tea, then asked, "Did you come across Sandra?"

"No."

"She's not upstairs," Vicki said. "I don't know where she could have got to."

Before they could discuss Sandra further, Alice came in with a large poppy seed cake which Moira had made earlier. While the maid was in the room, she twice caught Andrew's eye. He felt flattered that this attractive girl fancied him. But he was also embarrassed, in case Vicki noticed them exchanging glances. And he was concerned, remembering Alice's remark about "accidents" that morning. The next time that they were alone together, he must ask her what she meant by it.

Paul joined them and they sat, making conversation, drinking tea and eating cake. After a while, Lord Hetherington came down, apologized to Andrew for giving him a scare and assured the others that he was well. He even played a game of chess with Paul.

Sandra didn't appear, however, and Vicki's father was feeling tired, so he suggested that they postpone their family meeting until the next day.

It was a cosy domestic scene. The Hetheringtons

looked like a perfectly normal family, Andrew thought, who were coping well with their bereavement.

Too well.

9

At breakfast the next day, Andrew and Alice exchanged friendly smiles, but Vicki was there throughout, and seemed in an odd mood, so Andrew thought it best not to make conversation with the maid.

"Don't you find it odd?" he said to Vicki later that morning. "Having servants who are practically the same age as you?"

"Who? Alice? I'm not used to her yet, I must admit," Vicki said, confusing him. "I expect that you find the whole concept of having servants odd. For me, it's the other way round – I've only just got used to cooking and cleaning for myself in the flat at college. The other girls think I'm a terrible slob."

Sandra hadn't shown up for breakfast. Andrew gathered that she rarely did. No one seemed terribly worried.

"She wasn't around when I looked for her earlier," Vicki said, "but her bed was slept in last night. I checked."

"Does she often behave like this?"

"She sometimes stays on the second floor for days on end," Vicki admitted. "You hear her creaking about at night, but if you go and seek her out she's liable to fly into a rage. She sneaks into the kitchen. Once she ate an entire family picnic Moira had prepared the night before. After her midnight feasts she goes back upstairs and makes herself sick."

"But she looks so healthy at the moment."

"That's because she's on one of her exercise binges. They last up to a month. She has them once or twice a year." Vicki sighed. "Hopefully, she'll be normal enough to go to Mummy's funeral."

"Isn't it about time you told me what … happened to Sandra?" Before Vicki could answer this question, McFadyen appeared.

"Excuse me, Mr Andrew, Miss Victoria. Have you seen Alice? She's meant to be helping Moira."

"Not since we finished breakfast," Andrew told McFadyen.

"I'll remind her if we do," Vicki said.

As McFadyen went out, Lord Hetherington came in.

"I was wondering if you'd seen Sandra," he said, "so that we can have the family conference we were meant to have last night."

"I'm sorry, no," Vicki said. "I could go up and look for her."

"Best not," her father said. "Best not. Incidentally, if one of you should happen to answer the phone and it's that doctor again, get me straight away, whatever I'm doing."

"I didn't know the phones were working," Vicki replied.

"According to McFadyen, there's nothing wrong with them."

Andrew was about to ask why Lord Hetherington didn't just ring the doctor back. But then Vicki's father spoke again, in a softer voice.

"By the way," he said, "I spoke to the undertaker this morning. Funeral's on Friday."

"Doesn't there have to be an inquest first?" Andrew asked.

"Yes. Tomorrow." Lord Hetherington looked at Vicki. "No need for you to come, my dear, but if Sandra shows up, remind her about the meeting, won't you?"

Vicki agreed that she would and Lord Hetherington went off to do whatever it was he did. Vicki's father seemed recovered from the attack he'd had the previous day, but he also gave the impression of a man with a lot on his mind.

Sandra didn't show up during the day. Nor did Alice, as far as Andrew could tell, though the maid's absence wasn't remarked on again. Vicki and her father seemed concerned about Sandra, but not in a big way. After dinner, Andrew, Vicki, Paul and Lord Hetherington watched a video: an interminable war film whose name Andrew never caught. Paul and his lordship were thoroughly absorbed. Andrew and Vicki held hands and watched politely.

The next day, Lord Hetherington went to Kelso for the inquest. Vicki and Andrew decided to explore the area by car. They drove to the coast, having a fish and chip lunch at Seahouses. It was too windy to walk on the beach, so they decided to leave the Farne Islands and Lindisfarne for another day.

On the way back they stopped off in Wooler, where they poked around an antique shop for half an hour. It was a relief to be away from Hetherington Hall. When they returned, both of them felt tired, but relaxed.

Andrew went up to his room. It was clear that Alice was still gone. She hadn't been there at breakfast and his bed hadn't been made. Funny how quickly you got used to having things done for you. He told Vicki, but she was more concerned about Sandra. She went up to the second floor after dinner, called her sister's name a few times and opened a couple of doors.

"If she's prone to odd behaviour, her mother dying can't have helped," Andrew said.

"I know," Vicki agreed. "Sandra was the only one of us who was really close to Mummy. It must have hit her harder than appeared at first." Her voice trailed off. "But I need to tell her about the funeral tomorrow," she added.

Andrew found it odd that somebody could just vanish in a house, even one of this size. Yet Vicki assured him that the second floor, in particular, was like a rabbit warren.

"If Sandra doesn't want to see anyone, she won't."

"Maybe we should go down to the kitchen at night, keep watch for her."

"No," Vicki said. "We'll let Sandra be. But let's go down to the kitchen and see Moira, anyway."

Moira was sitting by the stove, still wearing an apron, soaking her feet in an enamelled basin full of hot water.

"You poor thing," Vicki said. "Are you exhausted?"

"I'm not, but my feet are. Bring the sherry from the butler's pantry, dear. I've not had that Alice to fetch and carry for me today and I deserve a bonus."

"What do you think happened to Alice?" Vicki asked Moira.

"Now that's a mystery. She was always such a reliable girl."

Andrew found this answer odd, as Alice had told him that she'd only been working for the Hetheringtons for a couple of months. Why did Moira use the word "always"? But he said nothing. Vicki and Moira obviously had plenty to talk about.

At first, Vicki and Moira tried to include Andrew in their conversation. He, however, said little. Soon, the two women began to forget that he was there. As they drank the sweet sherry, Vicki and Moira began to discuss the old days, when Vicki was growing up in the hall.

It was interesting for Andrew to hear Vicki talking about her childhood, which she rarely discussed with him. She and Moira reminisced about the eccentricities of servants who used to work in the house. Several, he gathered, had been sacked because they didn't come up to Lady Hetherington's high standards. No direct words of criticism were uttered, but Andrew began to get a clearer picture of Vicki's parents: her father as an easygoing, affectionate father, but none too successful business-man; her mother as an ambitious, neurotic tyrant.

Not for the first time, he couldn't help wondering if someone had wanted her dead.

10

The funeral was a small family affair in a chapel a hundred metres from Hetherington Hall. The tiny chapel was even more badly in need of repair than the hall itself. Vicki told Andrew that the chapel used to host a weekly service for the family and servants, but the last one was before the Second World War.

The Hall's other outbuildings stood empty now, and, apart from the stables, which had been converted into a garage, were ramshackle and potentially dangerous. Next to the chapel was a cemetery which housed generations of Hetheringtons. A marble slab stood by the place where Vicki's mother was to be buried. It marked the graves of Vicki's grandfather and grandmother. Lord Hetherington was their only child.

Sandra didn't come to the funeral. Apart from the vicar, Paul, Vicki, her father and Andrew, there was only Moira, McFadyen and Mr Gallagher, the family solicitor. The friends of Lady Hetherington's débutante days had either deserted her, or not been informed of her ladyship's death. The service was over very quickly.

Afterwards, everyone hurried back to the Hall, but Andrew lingered. He felt out of place on this intimate family occasion. That was how he came to spot someone new approaching the cemetery after everyone else was out of sight. A woman with dark, familiar hair stood by Lady Hetherington's grave-side with a strange smile on her face. Sandra had made it to the funeral after all.

Having stood outside watching, Andrew was the last person back into the house. He walked into the hallway unheard, and was about to go into the sitting-room when he heard Lord Hetherington's voice. Andrew stopped, thinking for a moment that his lordship's words might be addressed to him.

"You're sure you won't stay for a drink and some-thing to eat?"

"No. Thank you. I have a lot of other business to attend to. Here are the papers you asked for," Mr Gallagher's voice replied.

"Thanks, Henry. I'll go over them and return everything next week. We'll discuss whatever alterations need making then."

"I must admit, Percy, that I'm nervous about all these documents being out of the office safe. If you would only allow me to make photocopies…"

"No. No copies. Once a copy exists, another can easily be made, then another. You understand?"

"Of course. You realize, though, that your will is among these documents. In essence, your wife's death doesn't change any of its provisions. Therefore I don't see the need…"

His lordship brushed these arguments aside.

"I'll see you next week, Henry. We'll sort it all out then." He began to usher the solicitor out. They walked straight past Andrew, too busy talking to notice him.

"By the way," Mr Gallagher said. "I've had Doctor Rutherford on the phone, asking after you. She said it's urgent that she talk to you, but there's been some fault on your line."

"How the deuce did she get your number?" Vicki's father asked, in an irritated voice. "She's meant to contact me directly. In fact, she rang here the other day, but we were cut off."

"If you remember, when…" They went outside and Andrew couldn't hear the rest.

Andrew joined Vicki and Moira, his head buzzing. As he sat down, Paul left the room.

"Where are you going?" Vicki asked.

"To look at my butterflies," Paul said.

"Poor lamb," Moira said when he'd gone,

"spending all his time with dead butterflies."

"He'll be back at school next week," Vicki said.

"And you think he's happy there?"

"I don't know," Vicki said. "I was."

Moira shook her head.

"Eventually you were, my dear, when you were twelve, or thirteen. Until then you were miserable. Why, when you came home, you used to come down to the kitchen and cry your little eyes out on my pinny."

Vicki didn't comment on this. Instead, she asked, "Does Paul have many friends at school, do you know?"

"I don't, dear. Why don't you ask him? I must be going." Moira left and Vicki took the hint she'd given.

"Have you seen the butterfly collection yet?" Vicki asked Andrew.

"No. Where's it kept?"

"In a special room in the cellar. The cold down there helps to keep them in perfect condition. I'm sure that Paul would love to show the collection to you."

Instead of going down by the servants' stairs, Vicki took Andrew down a staircase at the back of the house, the one he'd used on his first evening at the hall. This time, as they walked away from the kitchen, into the dark reaches of the cellar, Andrew was conscious of a loud, throbbing noise.

"What's that whirring?" he asked.

Vicki opened a door, revealing a massive metal contraption.

"The generator. We're too far out to have our own power lines."

"What powers the generator?"

"Oil. A tanker comes once a month. They pump the stuff in from the back of the house. The central heating boiler's in there, too."

"Perhaps we could turn it on," Andrew said.

Vicki smiled.

"It wouldn't make a lot of difference. Hetherington Hall is like a lot of old country houses. The family spent a fortune putting in central heating when it had only just been invented. Now it's completely out of date. The thing consumes gallons and gallons of oil and hardly has any effect on how hot the house is. But, needless to say, we can't afford to have it replaced. Come winter, we spend our entire lives wearing thick sweaters."

They went further into the cellars. Vicki showed Andrew the wine cellar, which was locked. Then they turned a corner and found themselves facing an iron door with an even more impressive lock.

"Better knock," Vicki said. "This is Paul's territory."

Andrew knocked. A couple of moments later, the door opened, slowly. Paul was still wearing the slightly too tight suit he'd put on for the funeral.

"Hi, Paul," Andrew said. "I was wondering if you'd show me the family butterfly collection."

The miserable expression on the boy's face seemed to dissolve, although he kept his voice flat and bored.

"OK," he said. "You may as well come in."

The room was square with a low ceiling. On every wall, from the floor to the very top, were wooden drawers, hundreds of them. In the centre of the room was a glass-topped table with a lamp above it. On closer examination, the top turned out to be backlit and the surface was a vast magnifying glass.

"My grandfather had this room made," Paul said.

"Are all the drawers full?"

"Nearly. Do you want to see?"

There are – Paul informed Andrew – about three hundred and eight species of butterfly in Europe alone. All of them were represented in the Hetherington collection. Each drawer held a species. Paul slid out glass trays which contained numerous subspecies of each butterfly. Andrew pulled out a drawer at random.

"What's this one?" He pointed at a butterfly whose label indicated it had been captured in Northumberland the year before. Its upperside was dark brown with silver-blue scales, while the underside was pale grey, with a kind of blue tint to it, and small white-ringed spots.

"It's a *Cupido Minimus*."

"Does it have an English name?"

"Do you mean proper name or a translation?"

"A proper name."

"They're called 'Little Blue', though the one you're pointing at isn't so little. Its forewing is nearly fourteen millimetres long. You only get them that size high up. I caught it in my summer holidays last year. Daddy said he'd never seen a bigger one. But they're very common. Let me show you something much rarer."

Paul produced an Andalusian Anomalous Blue, which he and his father had found on a holiday in Spain two years before.

"This one was only discovered in 1979 and it's very rare. Most collections don't have one. You can tell it mainly by the white stripe on the underwing."

They'd spent nearly an hour in the butterfly room before they were interrupted. Paul explained all of the parts of the butterfly to Andrew, then showed him what he thought of as the collection's highlights. From Vicki's bored yawn, Andrew gathered that she had never spent so long in here before. He was beginning to tire himself when, to their surprise, Lord Hetherington came in.

"Ah, I was beginning to wonder where you three were. You'll forgive me for deserting you earlier. I've been preoccupied with clearing up your mother's affairs. Most rude of me. Have you showed them our *Agrodiaetus Violetae*, eh, Paul?"

"The Andalusian Blue. Yes, Daddy."

"Good, good. You know, I've always meant to write a book about butterflies. Maybe it's something Paul and I can do together, when he's older." He smiled, a man at ease with his family. "Time for lunch," he added.

The four of them went upstairs. Despite the cake an hour before, everyone was hungry. The morning's funeral already seemed forgotten.

11

"Is there any word about Alice?" Andrew asked Lord Hetherington as they were finishing lunch.

Vicki's father grunted a negative and started a conversation with Paul about butterfly hunting. Andrew said nothing, but his opinion of Lord Hetherington began to fall. How could Vicki's father care more for butterflies than for a human being?

The more he thought about it, what kind of person collected butterflies, anyway? He could understand why someone collected things which they could use, like books or CDs. He could almost understand why people might collect things which they could only look at, like postcards, or postage stamps. But butterflies? Beautiful creatures which have once been alive and which you have to kill to preserve? After an hour looking at them in that cold, catalogued room, Andrew found the idea more and more repugnant.

When he and Vicki were finally on their own in her bedroom, he told her his feelings. His girlfriend agreed with him.

"I can happily watch butterflies in the air outside, fluttering over the heather. Looking at them under glass gives me the creeps. It was clever of you to show such interest, though. It got you into Paul and Daddy's good books. They like having you around."

"It wasn't as calculated as all that."

"No," Vicki said, kissing him. "Of course it wasn't."

Later, Vicki told Andrew some more about Paul — how when he was younger he was very sickly and spent a lot of time in hospital. At one point, he wasn't expected to survive.

"I'd like to see some pictures of you and Paul when you were younger," Andrew said. "Your father showed me stuff from generations back, but nothing recent."

"I don't remember very many photos being taken," Vicki said.

"I'd still like to see them," Andrew pressed her.

"There ... might be some more in the library."

"Why don't we go and look now?"

Vicki seemed reluctant. Andrew remembered that Lord Hetherington had used a key to get into the library. Maybe Vicki wasn't allowed in there. But, if so, why?

"Come on," he pressed. "We've got nothing better to do."

"Oh, all right," Vicki said.

He followed her down to the butler's pantry. McFadyen wasn't around, and Moira was absorbed in preparing dinner, so Vicki took the library key from one of the hooks on the inside of the pantry door.

"Why's it kept locked?" Andrew asked, as Vicki let them into the room. She didn't reply. Andrew went over and began looking through the leather-bound house books. They were roughly in order, but weren't indexed or labelled on the outside, so it was hard to find the newest ones. The most recent ones he found were from the early sixties.

"I don't know where the rest are," Vicki said.

Andrew had a good look round. There were some books of a similar shape and size pushed back on one of the very top shelves. He pointed.

"Could they be them?"

"I'll take a look." Vicki got some wooden steps to stand on and reached to the back of the shelf, which stood nearly three metres off the ground.

"Ow! What is that?" Vicki hurried down the steps holding a broken whisky glass. Blood was dripping from her hand.

"How did that get up there?" she asked. "Oh, God, I hope I haven't got blood on any of the books."

"Never mind the books," Andrew told her. "What about you? That's a nasty cut on your palm."

"You're right," Vicki said. "It hurts."

She was, Andrew saw now, losing a lot of blood. He pulled a handkerchief from his pocket to stem the flow. As he was giving it to her, Vicki's body crumpled. She'd fainted.

Andrew caught her and laid her on the wooden floor.

"Vicki! Wake up, Vicki!"

Blood dripped into the cracks between the boards. Vicki murmured something, but didn't wake. Andrew tied the handkerchief round her hand to close the cut the best he could, then rang for McFadyen. He sat on the floor by Vicki and waited for the butler to come, cradling her head on his thigh. Nothing happened. Andrew got up and rang the bell again. This time, when he went back to Vicki, she came round.

"I'm OK," she said. "It wasn't the pain. It was the sight of the blood."

"I've rung the bell twice to get McFadyen to bandage you up, but nobody's come."

"I guess we'll have to go and find some bandages ourselves."

They walked slowly down to the kitchen, where Moira fussed over Vicki and bandaged her hand.

"You have a little rest before dinner, dear. You've lost some blood and you'll be tired. I'm sure Andrew can find something to occupy himself."

"I'll be fine," Andrew said. "By the way, the blood's left a bit of a mess in the library. If you give me a cloth, I'll…"

"Don't you worry," Moira stopped him. "I'll clean that later. You take Vicki up to her room."

Andrew walked Vicki up by the servants' stairway. She looked done in. He put her to bed and she fell instantly asleep.

Andrew went to his own room. Another lump of plaster had fallen from the ceiling on to his bed. He brushed it off and did some thinking. Where was Alice? Why were the house books for the last thirty-odd years missing? And what was the cause of Lady Hetherington's death?

The more he thought about it, the more suspicious Vicki's mother's death seemed. Even with the rowing machine above, a fitting didn't suddenly fall like that. It would work its way loose over a long period. Somebody would notice and fix it. Unless…

Unless somebody went into the bathroom, loosened the screws to within a millimetre of the end of their thread, then went into Sandra's exercise room, took up the floorboards and removed the clips which held the wire.

No. It was more likely that they'd do it the other way round. Then they'd actually test the fall of the bar heater, making sure that it would land in the bath, making contact with water. Finally, they'd put it back up, just before Lady Hetherington took her bath.

There was a flaw in the argument, however. For it to work, the murderer would have to know that Sandra would do her rowing exercises at precisely the same time as her mother took her bath. Unless, that is, Sandra was the murderer...

Vicki's sister *could* have done it. Shortly after the "accident", she vanished. Why? In remorse, or shock, or because she was afraid of being arrested? But there was a problem with this theory. Of all the members of the family, Sandra was the only one who seemed to get on with Lady Hetherington. If it *was* murder, why did she do it?

Sandra might be strange, but she still had to have some kind of motive. No matter how messed up Sandra was, on the brief occasions when Andrew had met her, she seemed rational enough. She would only do something for a reason. Perhaps the motive lay in the problems of her past, which Vicki had hinted at. Or perhaps they lay in the missing house books in the library.

Andrew went back to Vicki's room to check that she was all right. She was still fast asleep. It was gone seven, but the dinner gong hadn't rung. Moira must be running late. He decided to risk going back to the library on his own.

Andrew hoped not to run into Lord Hetherington. Andrew was a guest in the house. No one had actually told him that there were certain rooms he could go into and certain ones he couldn't. Yet it seemed implicit that he was only meant to enter particular rooms by invitation, and the library was one of them. He half expected it to be locked, but the door remained open, as Vicky and he had left it two hours before.

Vicki's blood still stained the floor. Moira would find it hard to get out. Andrew climbed the wooden steps as she'd done earlier. He was taller than Vicki and could see the remains of the broken glass on the top shelf. Gingerly, he reached around them, pulling out the leather-bound volumes. The books were dusty, he realized, as he slid them into his hand. Yet no dust had gathered on the broken glass. Who had left it there? And when? And why?

Expectantly, Andrew took the house books to the big oak table in the centre of the library, and opened the first one. It was dated thirty years ago. He found a wedding photograph of Lord and Lady Hetherington. It was true: Vicki's mother was once a beauty. There were various clippings from newspapers, and a list of the friends and relatives who attended the wedding. Again he wondered why none of these people had turned up for her funeral.

Andrew turned the pages and realized, suddenly, that the book had been badly mutilated. A lot of things were still there – he found, for instance, Vicki's first school report, and an account of Lord Hetherington employing Moira "after a satisfactory interview with her ladyship" – but a lot of things weren't. There were glue marks where clippings or photographs had been removed. As the book went on, whole pages had been torn out. He could find no trace of Vicki's birth, nor that of her elder sister. The last section of the book had been removed completely.

Andrew turned to the next book, the one which should have documented the last ten years.

Its pages were completely blank.

12

"I hadn't realized how tired I was," Vicki said when she came down for dinner at eight. "I've been sleeping badly," she explained. "I keep waking in the night, thinking I hear noises."

Lord Hetherington was quiet during dinner, a rabbit stew, which Moira served on her own. It must have been McFadyen's night off, Andrew decided. They drank the Châteauneuf-du-Pape which his lordship had brought up from the wine cellar, finishing the bottle before Moira produced the meal's crowning glory, a bread and butter pudding.

"Is tonight a good time for our family meeting?" Vicki asked, as they drained their coffees.

Lord Hetherington looked awkward.

"Are you recovered from your accident, earlier?"

he asked, in a tone which suggested that this wasn't the real reason for his reluctance. Andrew felt they wanted him out of the way. He had yet to tell anyone about the mutilated books in the library, but now didn't seem like a good time.

"If you'd like me to leave," he said, "I'd quite understand."

"I'm sure you do understand, Andrew," Vicki's father said slowly, "that some matters are best kept private. What I want to discuss, however, can only be broached when Sandra is here. After all, she's ... the eldest."

"Does that mean I can leave the table?" Paul asked.

"Of course, old chap, if that's what you want."

Paul got up and started rummaging in a corner. Lord Hetherington started up a forced conversation about Andrew's art course. Then Andrew managed to get in a question about the missing maid.

"Have you rung her home?" he enquired of Lord Hetherington.

"I think McFadyen did the day she disappeared," his lordship replied, in an off-hand manner. "They didn't know what had happened to her. But the phones are still on the blink and her family are farmers – you can only catch them in at certain times. I'm sure there's nothing to be concerned about."

Andrew wasn't so sure, but it was clear that Lord

Hetherington didn't want to discuss the matter further.

"You must be concerned about Sandra, though?" he commented. Lord Hetherington nodded.

"Yes. But it's not the first time she's behaved in this way."

Andrew decided that it was time to broach the question which Vicki had refused to answer earlier in the week.

"How did it happen?" he asked. "What made Sandra the way she is?"

"She was supposed to marry," Lord Hetherington said, in a cold voice. "But it went tragically wrong." He paused, but his chilly expression told Andrew not to attempt any more questions.

"I think," Lord Hetherington went on, "that I ought to go up and find Sandra now. I shall try to persuade her to come down for a family meeting, tomorrow afternoon. If she won't come, we will hold the meeting without her, at two. There are things we have to discuss which won't wait any longer."

Paul put down his Nintendo and helped his father out of the room.

"He suddenly looks very old," Vicki said.

"What do you think he wants to talk to you about?" Andrew asked, now they were alone. From her awkward responses earlier, he judged it safest not to ask any more questions about Sandra's wedding for a while.

"Money, I suppose. He's been strapped for cash for years. Paul's school fees can't be helping. You know, Daddy only does the most essential repairs to the house, but even so, as you can imagine, it costs a fortune to run."

"Aren't there things that he can sell?"

Vicki shrugged.

"Some furniture, maybe. The wine cellar. All the good paintings went years ago. The only ones left are portraits which are worth less than they'd cost to restore."

"So what is there to discuss?"

Vicki measured her words carefully.

"Daddy always expected to die before Mummy did. Now all that's changed. Paul is the heir, because he's male, but he can't manage the Hall until he's twenty-one."

"That's not fair, is it?" Andrew commented. "Why should it be the boy who inherits, succeeds to the title?"

"It's just the way things are," Vicky said. "It makes no difference to me, anyway. If it was the eldest who inherited, I'd still miss out. What I care about is us keeping the Hall, and the land around it. Does that sound awful to you? Do you believe in inherited wealth?"

"Not really. But if I'd grown up in a place like this…" Vicki didn't let Andrew finish the thought.

"You see, I might not end up working round here,

or even living here, but I want to always be able to come back when I feel like it. I want my own children to have what I had."

"You think there's a risk of your father selling up completely?" Andrew asked.

Vicki nodded.

"Daddy's made some bad investments over the years. I guess a lot depends on what he was doing in South Africa. He's bound to tell us about that at the meeting tomorrow."

"About Sandra…" Andrew began.

"I don't want to talk about Sandra now," Vicki said. "That was tactless of you, to bring it up at the dinner table, when Paul was still in the room. Daddy was embarrassed."

Taken aback by the anger in her voice, Andrew waited before telling Vicki about what he'd found in the house books while she slept. When he did, Vicki shrugged and said it didn't make sense. She didn't seem interested. Andrew could tell that his girl-friend was holding something back, but she was in a bad mood, so he didn't challenge her. They played an endless game of Trivial Pursuit.

Later, going back to his room at midnight, Andrew thought he heard steps on the stairway. Perhaps, he thought, Sandra was sneaking down to the kitchen, getting herself something to eat. He stood on the landing, hoping to get a glimpse of her.

But it wasn't Sandra. It was Paul, in pyjamas and bare feet. He nearly bumped into Andrew as he hurried on to the landing on the way back to his bedroom. The boy scurried off without speaking.

13

The next day it turned cold, but the heating wasn't switched on. Andrew found it hard to get out of bed. Eventually, though, he put on his one warm sweater and went down for breakfast, very late. Vicki was waiting for him. She hadn't eaten yet, either. Andrew rang the bell, but McFadyen didn't appear.

"I hope he hasn't vanished too," Andrew quipped to Vicki. The look on Vicki's face told him that she didn't appreciate the joke. They went to the kitchen and got some muesli and orange juice. The stove had been on and it was warmer there than in the breakfast room, so they decided to stay in the kitchen while they ate.

Moira wasn't around either, so Vicki made a pot of tea herself.

"I often had breakfast down here with Moira when I was home from school," she said.

"Why not with your parents?"

"Daddy was away a lot. Mummy and I were never that close. She always spent a lot more time with Sandra than with me."

Andrew finished his muesli, which was dry and rather stale.

"Where do you think Moira is?"

"Probably cleaning somewhere."

"I've been thinking," Andrew said, "about Alice. Has there been any word from her?"

"I only know what Daddy said at dinner last night," Vicki told him. "He deals with matters to do with the servants."

"But suppose something's happened to her?"

"Then her parents would have called, or the police. Why are you so bothered about her?"

Andrew didn't reply at once. He didn't know how much Vicki had noticed the undercurrent of desire between him and the maid. But that wasn't the only reason for his concern. Alice's absence on its own might not have worried him, but following so soon after Lady Hetherington's violent death, it seemed ominous. Without answering Vicki's question, he pressed his point.

"The phones here keep going out of action.

Someone could have been trying to call. Where does she live? Nearby?"

"Her family farm's about five miles away."

"Why don't we go and visit her?"

"I don't see the…"

"Just for a minute or two, to set my mind at rest. Then you could show me some more of the area." Andrew gave Vicki a warm smile, to show that he wasn't getting at her. Reluctantly, she conceded.

"If we're going to go, we'd better get a move on, or we won't be back in time for lunch."

It was nearly eleven. They took the servants' stairs up to the main hall. Vicki was right. Moira had been cleaning. The doors to nearly all of the rooms off the hall were open and a vacuum cleaner stood outside the sitting-room. But it wasn't switched on. Andrew could hear Moira's voice, coming from the one room whose door wasn't open.

"Which room is that?" he asked Vicki.

"My father's study."

While Vicki went to get the car, Andrew stood in the hall, listening.

"…finished," Moira said, angrily. "I don't blame him. I've been a fool to stay all these years, haven't I? And now it's all crumbling down around you."

Vicki's father replied in a softer, placatory tone. The only words which Andrew could make out were "all right".

"No," Moira replied. "It won't be all right.

That's what I'm trying to tell you. All you can think about is your plans for Paul. It's too late for Sandra, but what about Vicki?"

Andrew couldn't hear the reply, but what Moira said next sent a chill down his neck.

"That's all very well, but there's her boyfriend, too. He's not all he seems. Have you taken a close look at him?"

Andrew heard the sound of a car horn. He waited to hear what Moira said next, but Lord Hetherington was talking about McFadyen and something to do with money. The car horn sounded again and Andrew went out to join Vicki.

Andrew was relieved to be out of the house at last. It was a chilly, windy day, but an attractive one. Clouds scudded across the sky and the cotton grass bent in the stiff breeze. Despite her bandaged hand, Vicki insisted on driving. As they got away from the Hall, she seemed to relax a little.

"If we're going to her house," Vicki said, "I suppose I ought to tell you about me and Alice, before she does."

"What do you mean?"

"There was a time," Vicki said, without taking her eyes off the road, "when I used to play with Alice. She's eighteen months younger than me, but she was the only girl anywhere near my age for twenty miles or so. Daddy used to send the Bentley and have her brought up to the house."

Andrew was surprised that Vicki hadn't mentioned this before.

"Did you get on well?"

Vicki shook her head.

"Towards the end I used to bully her terribly. Not let her use my toys, insist that she did all the tidying up, that sort of thing. I don't know why. When I was Paul's age, I turned into a pretty horrible child. I'd grown out of it by the time I was a teenager, but, by then, the age difference mattered too much. Alice and I never made it up."

"She must have been very cheesed off with you."

Vicki looked embarassed.

"Alice used to let me boss her about. She didn't have friends outside school either, the family farm being very remote. So she tried to hang on to me until I dropped her." She paused, then asked, "Do you hate me?"

"Of course not," Andrew said. "But I can see why Alice might. How long has she worked in the Hall?"

"Only since the summer. Mummy took her on, knowing full well how uncomfortable it would make me."

"Have you spoken to her much since we've been here?"

"Are you kidding?" Vicki pulled up outside a small stone farmhouse.

"You remembered the way," Andrew said.

"Of course I did. This used to be part of the

Hetherington estate," Vicki explained. "I suspect Dad sold it to Alice's father because he needed the money for my school fees."

As they got out, Vicki put her bandaged hand on Andrew's arm.

"Can you do the talking?"

A woman in dungarees came to the door. She eyed Vicki and Andrew suspiciously.

"And what can I do for you?"

Andrew suddenly realized the delicacy of the situation they were in. If Alice's mother didn't know that she had disappeared, he might throw her into a panic.

"It's about Alice," he said.

The woman shook her head angrily.

"She's not coming back, if that's what you're after. Not even if..." She was interrupted by her daughter. Andrew was relieved to hear Alice's voice.

"It's OK, Mum. I'm a big girl now. I'll talk to them."

"All right," Alice's mother said. "But don't you let that Victoria talk you into anything. I've got to see to the pigs." Alice's mother pushed past them. Alice stared calmly at Vicki and Andrew.

"You'd better come in," she said.

The room was small but cosy. There was a wood fire burning in the grate. Alice motioned them to sit on the sofa while she stood by the fire. Vicki stayed standing.

103

"We were worried about you," Andrew said. "Vanishing like that."

"Who said I vanished?"

"Everyone," Andrew told her. "Moira. McFadyen."

"McFadyen knew why I went. He won't have said anything in front of you for fear of upsetting the apple cart. After all, he was in the same boat as me – at least that's what he said. Did you ask his lordship?"

"Well…"

Alice looked at Vicki.

"He's a slippery old sod, isn't he, your father? There are some stories I could tell."

"How dare you?" Vicki said, testily. "You've no right."

"This is my house which my family own," Alice snapped. "I've got every right to say what I want to in it."

"Then I'm not listening to you." Vicki walked out of the room without a backward glance.

"We didn't come to argue," Andrew said, standing up slowly. "We were both worried about what had happened to you."

"Have you come to pay her?" Alice's mother had come back into the room.

"Pay?" Andrew said, weakly. He was working out what should have been clear to him days ago.

"She's owed six weeks' wages. That's why she's left. That new butler kept making excuses, so she

104

went to see his lordship as soon as he got home. Fat lot of good it did her. He claimed to be broke, told her he'd have plenty of money by next week. Have you brought the money?"

"I'm afraid…"

"I'm not surprised. You'd better get out before your girlfriend drives off without you."

Alice defended Andrew.

"This has nothing to do with him, Mum. It's not his fault his girlfriend treated me like muck when I was a kid, or that her father gave me the only job I could get then treated me like muck, too. Leave him be."

"Thanks for defending me," Andrew said to Alice. "But I'd better go."

The girl gave him a tender, admiring look.

"You seem like a nice bloke," she said. "I don't know what you're doing with *Miss* Victoria, I really don't."

"Maybe she's changed since you knew her," Andrew muttered, then added: "What will you do if you're not going back to the Hall?"

"Work on the farm," Alice said. "There's plenty of work – just no money to pay me with. But it's experience, I suppose. I've applied to go to Sutton Bonnington Agricultural College next year." She smiled at Andrew as if to say, "You see, I'm not just a maid." Andrew went to the door, then turned back.

"You said you had some stories to tell. Were any of them about Vicki's sister, Sandra?"

Alice smiled.

"The crazy sisters," she said.

Andrew ignored the jibe against Vicki.

"Do you know who Sandra was supposed to marry?"

"They keep that quiet, do they?" Alice's mother said, coming back into the room. "I'm not surprised. I'll tell you who Sandra was going to marry: Charles Partington. Have you heard of him?"

"Was he from round here?" Andrew asked.

"He was. You ask Lord Hetherington what happened to Charles Partington. Go on, ask him."

Andrew wanted to question her further but, at that moment, Vicki sounded the horn on the car. Reluctantly, he went out to join her.

14

"**D**amn!" Vicki said, a couple of minutes after they'd left Alice.

"What's wrong?" Andrew asked. Then the spluttering noise made by the engine rendered his question redundant.

"I meant to get some petrol in Wooler the other day, but I forgot."

The engine spluttered again and died.

"How far are we from the Hall?" Andrew asked.

"At least seven miles by car. Maybe five over the fields."

"We could go back to Alice's farm," he suggested, "scrounge some petrol from them."

"You're kidding, aren't you?" Vicki said. "After the way they treated me?"

"Oh, come on," Andrew said. "From what you told me, Alice has every reason to dislike you and your family. I'll go alone, if you like."

"No!" Vicki said. "I'd rather walk."

"All right," Andrew said. "We'll walk back to the Hall. It'll only take a couple of hours. McFadyen can come back in the Bentley and bring some petrol."

As he said this last sentence, it occurred to Andrew that he hadn't seen McFadyen since the funeral. Alice said he hadn't been paid. Suppose he, too, had walked out?

"I'll be late for the family meeting," Vicki said.

"They won't start without you," Andrew assured her. "It can't be helped." He got out of the car, then went round to her side.

"Take the hand brake off. You steer, and I'll push the car into the side of the road so that tractors can get by."

They moved the car then set off over the fields. The day was cold and windy. They weren't dressed for the open air, but there was no choice. Vicki seemed preoccupied. Andrew decided not to tell her that he'd discovered who Sandra was meant to marry. It could wait.

"Is this your land?" he asked Vicki, as they made their way through the purple heather.

"Some of it is," she replied, shivering a little. "I don't know the precise boundaries – anyway, we wouldn't be trespassing. There's a public right of way through all of it. Some agreement with the National Trust."

Andrew looked around at the rolling hills and the vast, unpeopled places beneath. Yes, he thought, this land ought to belong to everyone.

They walked mostly in the valleys, passing a few sheep, a river, a tree plantation, but no people. Andrew had read somewhere that Northumberland was the last wild place in England. Maybe it was true. He and Vicki walked in silence, holding hands except where it was too steep to keep their balance. They had been walking for an hour when Andrew spotted a trail snaking around a hill.

"What's that?" he asked Vicki.

"What does it look like?"

"A road."

"That's what it is."

"Where does it lead?"

Vicki paused.

"A family called the Partingtons used to live there. That road leads to their house."

"I'd like to see it."

"It's not on our way home," Vicki said, tetchily.

"A few minutes won't make any difference."

"It'd take more than a few minutes," Vicki said, "and, anyway, it's a ruin. There's nothing to see."

"I like ruins."

"Well, I don't want to go there."

"Why not?"

"If you must know," Vicki said, looking away from him, "the place gives me the creeps. There was a bad accident there. People died."

"How did it happen, the accident?" Andrew asked.

Vicki's voice became impatient.

"An electrical fault. Look, if you really want to go there, let's make it another day. OK?"

"OK." Andrew was about to ask another question when Vicki remembered something. She swore.

"What is it?"

"I left the keys in the car."

"Not too many car thieves round here, I'd have thought."

"I guess not," Vicki said. "Who'd want my old Mini anyway? We'll go straight back for it after lunch."

The weather had turned colder and the only way to stay warm was to walk quickly. Andrew began to feel very hungry. As the Hall came into sight, all he could think about was how a bowl of Moira's pea and ham soup would warm them both up.

They walked into the Hall through the front door. Everything was the way they'd left it. The vacuum cleaner stood exactly where it had been three hours before. A two-day-old copy of *The Scotsman* sat on the table by the phone. Vicki went into the sitting-room and rang the bell. Then, when no one came, she went to her father's study, knocked on the door and, when there was no reply, went in. Andrew waited a moment, then followed her. The study was an untidy room, with two filing cabinets and loose papers everywhere. It was empty.

"Where is everybody?" Vicki asked, aloud.

Andrew picked up the phone on Lord Hetherington's desk. The line was dead.

"Let's go down to the kitchen," he suggested.

If they were expecting to find Moira there, they were disappointed. Andrew looked in the pantry, and found them a banana each. They ate hungrily.

"What do you think's going on?" Vicki asked, as Andrew put the skins into the bin.

"I've no idea. They can't all be out. Where shall we look?"

"The first floor, I guess."

They took the servants' stairs up to the first floor, then walked around shouting.

"Hallo. Is anybody there? Hallo?"

There was no reply. They got to Paul's room. There was no sign of him. Next, they went to Lord Hetherington's bedroom, which Andrew hadn't been in before. It was a large, ornate room, with a four poster bed and a coal fire in the grate, unlit. It was also empty.

"What are we going to do?" Vicki asked.

Andrew had to admit that he had no idea.

"This is freaky," Vicki said. "I've never, ever been in the house on my own before."

"You're not alone now," he told her.

They hugged. Vicki was still shivering.

"I'm afraid," she said. "Aren't you?"

"Not yet," Andrew said.

What was making her afraid? Andrew hadn't told Vicki his suspicions that her mother had been murdered. He hoped that he was wrong about that. After all, Alice's disappearance turned out to have a simple, if depressing, explanation.

Vicki broke away from him.

"I think we should get out of here," she said. "I know where Daddy keeps the spare set of keys for the Bentley."

There was a bureau in the corner of the bedroom. Vicki opened one of the drawers and pulled out the keys.

"But where should we go?" Andrew asked.

"The police."

"Isn't that overreacting? What's the crime?"

"I don't know. Daddy's solicitor, then: Mr Gallagher."

Andrew tried to calm Vicki down.

"Maybe we're panicking too quickly. There's probably a perfectly simple explanation. Where's the garage?"

"The old stables round the back. There's a door near the library."

They hurried out. Andrew glanced into the library as they left. No one was in there. Vicki's blood – dry, now – still stained the wooden floor.

"Here," Vicki said, handing him the key to the garage. "Can you open this? My hands are shaking."

Andrew took the key, but when they got to the garage, he didn't need it. The stable doors, like the rest of the doors in the house, had been left wide open. There was no car inside.

"Now are you afraid?" Vicki asked.

.

15

Storm clouds gathered overhead. The nearest building was Alice's farm, a good three hours' walk away. Andrew told Vicki that her father and brother were bound to come back, but she wasn't convinced.

"He's gone," she said, her voice rising anxiously. "The servants have walked out and Daddy's taken Paul and left. Paul's the only one he really cared about – the male heir he waited so long for. Daddy must have gone bust. That was what the family meeting was going to be about."

Vicki seemed on the verge of hysteria. Andrew remembered what Alice had said about the "mad sisters". Was Vicki secretly as unstable as Sandra? Andrew couldn't believe it. He tried to calm her down.

"There's bound to be a simple explanation."

"Sure," said Vicki. "Maybe Daddy's creditors are about to seize the house and he's done a runner. I'll be penniless."

"Would that be so bad?" Andrew asked, trying to comfort her. "Look at the other people at college. They haven't got money behind them. They have to get by on their wits, on their qualifications."

"It's not the money I'm bothered about," Vicki said. "We've always been short of money. It's my home. How can you let somebody take away your home?"

"You can even get used to not having a home," Andrew told her.

"I'm sorry," Vicki said, more tenderly. "I was so wrapped up in myself that I forgot. But what are we going to do now?"

Andrew thought for a moment. "I think we ought to search the house from top to bottom."

"What are we looking for?"

"Something. Anything that'll give us a clue as to what happened to the others."

"You know what gets me?" Vicki said.

"What?"

"Moira not being here. I can understand McFadyen walking out. He's only been with the family for a few months. But Moira's been with us for more than half her life – for all of mine. Even if she hadn't been paid for weeks, like Alice, I can't

believe that she'd just walk out like that. We were ...
are close."

"Maybe she's with Sandra."

"I doubt it. Sandra and her never got on that
well."

"Why don't we check her room? That'll tell us if
she's left."

"I guess," Vicki said. "Yes. We'll start there."

"Where are the servants' rooms? I've never seen
them."

"No," Vicki told him. "You wouldn't have."

In the mid-nineteenth century, Vicki explained,
when Hetherington Hall was built, the fashion
among the highest gentry was for servants to be seen
as little as possible. Therefore, separate passageways
were created for the servants to use when they
moved from one part of the house to another.

"So the house is full of secret passages?"

"They're not secret if you know what you're
looking for. The doorways are concealed behind
some of the wooden panels in the corridors. There
are also two staircases meant for servants: the one
we've just used, which leads from the main part of
the house into the kitchen, and another one, which
goes up from the back of the butler's pantry. We
haven't used that before because the only place it
goes to is the servants' living quarters."

They walked down to the kitchen and into the
butler's pantry. At the side of this recess was the

board where the bells rang. It looked like a complex kind of board game or early pin table, and bore the name: Edmunson's Electricity Corporation, Westminster. Most of the bedrooms were numbered. Andrew couldn't tell which was which. There were bells for the "boudoir" and the "white dressing-room", amongst others. Andrew wondered how many of these rooms were still used at all.

"Come on."

They climbed the staircase behind the pantry. Andrew realized that this was where he'd heard voices coming from on his first night in the Hall. McFadyen and Moira would have been talking to each other in their private quarters. He and Vicki walked up to the first floor, where there were just two rooms leading off the stairway: one to the left and one to the right. A third door was up a few more steps. It was locked.

"Where does this one lead?" Andrew asked Vicki.

"To the next floor. In the old days, most of the servants would have lived in the small rooms up there. Only the two most senior servants – the butler and his wife in those days – would get the bigger rooms on this floor. There never used to be any heating on the top floor, either. I guess the door's been locked for years."

Andrew tried the door to his right. It opened.

"This is McFadyen's room," Vicki told him.

"Not any more."

The room was empty. It had been meticulously cleaned out. No traces of the butler remained.

"It looks like he's done a bunk," Andrew said. "Presumably for the same reason as Alice."

Vicki nodded agreement. She tried the remaining door. It opened.

"This is Moira's room," she said.

Moira's room was bigger than the butler's, and crammed with things: a chest, a dressing table, a wardrobe, a TV set, and a small desk. There was no need to open any of the drawers to see if Moira had cleared them. They were overflowing. The room told a story of a full life lived in a small space. On the desk was a photo of Vicki, when she was maybe five years old, the only early picture of her which Andrew had seen. She was sitting on the housekeeper's lap, a smiling, innocent child.

"Fancy Moira having this," Vicki said, picking it up. "I've never seen it before. I don't remember her ever having her hair that way. Doesn't she look pretty?"

"So do you," Andrew said. "Anyway, your fears must be groundless. Moira hasn't cleared off, like Alice, or McFadyen. Though I suppose she could be with McFadyen."

"I don't give a stuff about McFadyen," Vicki said.

"But maybe Moira does," Andrew suggested. "Think about it. She's fortyish, and single. He must be about the same age, and I didn't see a wedding ring. It would be natural if…"

"I don't think so," Vicki said. "Let's brave the second floor, shall we?"

They went back through the kitchen and up the servants' stairway to the second floor. Vicki began calling out names.

"Paul?"

"Sandra?"

"Daddy?"

"Moira?"

There was no response. Next, they began opening doors. The last time Andrew saw Lord Hetherington, he was climbing up to this floor, looking for his eldest daughter. Andrew wondered if he'd found her.

They looked first in the exercise room. It was empty, the equipment unmoved since the last time Andrew had been in there.

"Let's try her bedroom," Vicki said.

Andrew would never have thought that the next room they went into was a bedroom. True, it had a single mattress on the floor. The rest of the floor was uncarpeted and covered with cheap, faded women's magazines, many of them cut or torn up. Amongst the copies of *Hello* and *Cosmopolitan* he spotted issues of *The Bride* and *Wedding World* with cover dates ten years old. Andrew was about to leave when he spotted a door, leading off from the bedroom.

"What's through there?"

"It's Sandra's dressing-room. I've never been allowed in it."

"Come on."

They went into the dark, narrow room. Andrew fumbled for a light switch.

"I feel like I'm breaking her trust, coming in these rooms," Vicki said. "She never lets anyone in here, not even Mummy."

"I'm surprised she's got so many clothes," Andrew said, opening one wardrobe, then another. "You said she hardly ever goes out."

"Most of these are ancient," Vicki pointed out. "Look at the styles."

Andrew was about to open the final wardrobe when there was what sounded like an enormous explosion.

"Only thunder," Vicki said. "The storm must have started." There was no window they could go to in the dressing-room, but Vicki was right. There was another loud thunderclap, followed by the sound of heavy rain. In the next moment, Andrew could have sworn that he heard something running across the floor above them. He immediately thought of Vicki's brother, preserving butterflies.

"Is that Paul, do you think?"

"I doubt it," Vicki said. "Probably a mouse, running from the rain. The roof leaks."

As Andrew opened the third wardrobe, he smelt something sickly, and sweet, something almost rotten. Then, before he could see what it was, the lights went out.

16

"A power failure," Vicki said. "That's all. It happens all the time."

"What do we do?"

"Wait for it to come back on. But let's get to some light." They felt their way out into the bedroom. Andrew could see the dark sky through dirty windows. A bolt of lightning struck the chapel, illuminating the gravestones around it.

"Look!" he said. "There's someone there."

But the light had gone and Vicki missed it.

"Either it's a fuse, or the generator's turned itself off," she told Andrew.

"Does it often do that?"

"Sometimes. It's an old system. I know how to work it. We'll wait for the storm to pass, then I'll go down and start it up. I'll put the heating on at the same time. I'm freezing."

"Me too."

They huddled together in the creepy room.

"Who did it look like?" Vicki asked Andrew. "In the cemetery?"

"I'm not sure," he replied. "It was only for a second or two. It might have been Paul."

"What would Paul be doing out there?"

"What would *anyone* be doing out there?"

"I don't like it up here," Vicki said. "I want to go downstairs. There's a fire in my room. We could light it."

"Sounds like a good idea to me."

They stumbled down the stairs at the side of the house and found their way to Vicki's dark room. Vicki lit a candle. Andrew watched as she made up the fire, a ghostly figure in the half light, adding wood to the tight coils of newspaper which were already in the grate.

"We'll be in trouble if the storm goes on for too long," she said, as deep red flames filled the room with an eerie light. "There's only enough wood to last an hour or so."

But the storm went on and on. They sat by the fire, not wanting to put voice to the dark thoughts going through their heads. At least the crackling and spluttering of the fire blocked out whatever other noises filled the old house. Andrew didn't believe in ghosts, but Hetherington Hall was the sort of place which could change anyone's mind. The fire waned, and the wood ran out. The room became cold again. They got under the covers of Vicki's bed to keep warm. Then, tired from their long walk earlier, they fell asleep.

When they woke, hours later, the storm had passed. It was evening. The sky was nearly clear, but what little light there was had already begun to drain from it.

"We'd better go downstairs," Vicki said, "sort out the power before the house is completely dark."

They made their way down to the cellar, carrying candles. By now, they'd given up expecting to meet anyone else in the house, so no longer called out names as they walked downstairs. The cellar was cold and dark. Andrew was glad that they didn't have to go too deeply into it. Vicki changed a fuse, but nothing happened. Then she played about with the pilot light and pulled a lever. There was a cranking noise and a shuddering and the generator whirred back into life. The light in the room came on.

"Now all I have to do is switch on the heating," Vicki said. She went over to the thermostat and paused. "That can't be right."

"What is it?"

She pointed at the fuel gauge. It was touching "empty".

"It never goes down this low."

"When does the oil tanker come?"

"At the end of every month, but the fuel never goes below a quarter full, not even in the winter. The tanker can't have been for at least two months, probably three." She paused and shook her head. "The money situation must be even worse than I thought. No wonder Daddy hasn't had the heating on. The fuel could run out at any moment. Then we won't have any lights or power of any kind. We'd better hurry upstairs, turn off as many things as possible. That way, we can make what little there is left last a bit longer."

As they hurried up the stairs back into the house, Andrew thought he heard something: a distant shout, or scream. He stopped and listened, but all that he could make out was the loud whirring of the generator. Still, as he walked back into the now brightly lit Hall, he couldn't help feeling that someone, somewhere, was calling for help.

They walked around the ground floor, candles in hand, turning off lights. Andrew tried the phone. It was still dead. Vicki joined him in the hallway.

"What do we do now?" she said.

Andrew didn't hesitate to say what he really thought.

"Every instinct tells me to get out of here."

"I can't do that," Vicki said. "This place is my home. It's my inheritance. I need to find out what's going on."

"All right," Andrew responded. "Where do we start looking?"

Vicki thought for a moment.

"Daddy's study," she said. "That's where he keeps all the financial papers."

Andrew remembered something else – how Mr Gallagher had given Lord Hetherington various papers, including the will, straight after the funeral. Would they be in his study, too? And why had Vicki's father wanted them?

He didn't, however, tell Vicki about this, in case it worried her further. She'd just gone on about her "inheritance". What if her father had decided to cut her out of his will? Or what if there was nothing left for him to leave?

The study didn't look as though it had been tidied recently. Nor did it look like anyone had left it in a hurry, which Andrew found strange. There was a green wire tray, marked "pending". It contained Lord Hetherington's unopened mail: mostly bills, by the look of it. There was also a yellow tray, marked "current", containing correspondence that he was working on, and a third, blue tray, "outgoing", which contained letters waiting to be posted. Vicki went through the trays while Andrew searched the drawers of his desk, looking for something to shed light upon her predicament.

Lord Hetherington was the kind of person who kept everything. There were bank statements going back thirty years and numerous insurance documents. None of this stuff was in order, either. Eventually, Andrew managed to find the most recent – the insurance policies were all up to date, but his bank account was badly overdrawn. Credit card statements showed that Lord Hetherington was like his daughter – over his credit limit – only he had four cards and the limit on each was ten times the size of Vicki's.

Andrew looked in vain for his Lordship's will or any other legal documents. Maybe they were in the trays which Vicki was searching. Nor did he find anything which might have been removed from the house books in the library. The biggest drawer, however, contained a lot of family papers, the sort of things which would have found their way into the house book had Lord and Lady Hetherington been keeping them up to date. There was, for instance, McFadyen's letter of application for the post of butler, and the reference provided by his previous employer, a churchman called Cardinal Chambers. The butler might have been better off if he'd stayed where he was.

Vicki blew her nose and Andrew turned round. She was, he saw, in tears.

"What's wrong?" he asked, going over to her. "Tell me what's wrong."

"This." She handed him a letter, postmarked South Africa, which was where Lord Hetherington had just come back from.

"It arrived this morning," Vicki told Andrew. "It's the only piece of mail he's opened since he got home."

The letter said that Hetherington Hall and all attendant lands were being bought, for a seven figure sum, by a Mr Pik Brickell of Capetown. It seemed that Lord Hetherington had told Alice the truth when he said that he would soon have plenty of money.

"Does it say when he'll get the money?" Andrew asked Vicki. She shook her head.

"All that's here is bills, bills and more bills. The oil company. The Council tax. The bank, threatening to take him to court. American Express. Even the butcher's in Kelso."

Andrew told Vicki what he'd found about the overdraft and credit card bills.

"Where do you think he's gone?" he asked, when he'd finished.

"I suppose that Daddy's lying low somewhere until the money arrives and he can spend it. He must have taken Paul. Maybe Sandra too. I don't know about Moira. Maybe she's gone with him."

"In that case," Andrew wanted to know, "why was all her stuff left behind?"

"I don't know," Vicki said. "Maybe you're right, and she did leave with McFadyen, not realizing that the money really was coming this time."

"I don't think so," Andrew said. "She was still here this morning, whereas McFadyen was gone yesterday. Tell me, was the Bentley in the garage when you got the Mini out this morning?"

"Yes," Vicki said.

"So it must have been your father who took it, not McFadyen. But I still don't see why he'd have cleared off like that."

Vicki shrugged.

"He walked out on my mother enough times," she revealed.

"You never said."

Vicki shrugged despairingly.

"Nobody likes to tell tales on their own father. But there were affairs, when I was younger. And there've always been money troubles. I nearly had to leave school once because the bills hadn't been paid." She held up an envelope. "There's a letter from Paul's school here, 'reminding' Daddy that he still owes for last term."

"Why did things get so bad?" Andrew asked.

Vicki sighed.

"Daddy's never had a proper job. He's always lived on investments. And betting. But, as far as I can see, he's never been terribly good at either. Mummy had some money, I think, and inherited more when her parents died. But it's all gone now." She burst into tears again. "I can't believe he'd do that. I can't believe that he'd sell the roof from over our heads."

Andrew tried to comfort her.

"Maybe he had no choice."

"He didn't even consult us."

"I guess you were right earlier – that's what the family meeting was going to be about."

"I'm sure it was," Vicki said. "But if Daddy'd already decided what he was going to do, what difference would a meeting make?"

"Is the house definitely sold?"

Vicki looked at the letter from South Africa again.

"I don't know. It says here that there are some forms which he has to sign and take to his solicitor. I suppose that Daddy's taken them with him."

"Did you find any other papers?" Andrew asked.

"Like what?"

"His will, for instance."

"That's kept at the solicitors."

"I don't think so." Andrew explained what he'd overheard after the funeral the other day. Vicki thought about it.

"If he's selling the house and land, Daddy won't have anything to leave to anyone, except his title."

"There's the money from the house."

"He'll get through that in no time. He must owe half of it."

By now it was dark and too late to do anything else. The phone was still dead. They slept in the same room that night. At least, Vicki slept. Andrew lay awake, listening for noises and worrying about what was happening. What kind of family was this, which took death in its stride, then deserted their youngest daughter?

The house remained quiet. Still unable to sleep, Andrew decided to set aside his fears and go downstairs. He sat in the kitchen with a glass of milk, thinking. So many people were missing: Moira, Paul, Sandra, Vicki's father. He knew none of them well, yet found it hard to believe that they had all simply deserted the house. But what were the alternatives? All he could think of was this: *if they didn't leave of their own free will, someone must have got rid of them.*

How would they do that? They could have been scared away. Or…

Or he and Vicki were in great danger. He'd made a mistake. He should never have left Vicki alone, not for a minute.

Andrew hurried back upstairs to her room, slowing his footsteps down as he got nearer and treading gently so as not to wake her. He opened the door slowly, intending to sneak in without switching the light on. But when Andrew got inside, he saw that the bedside lamp was already lit. Vicki's bed was empty.

She was gone.

17

Andrew tried to think. It was just after midnight. He had been out of the room less than ten minutes. He told himself that Vicki could have gone to the bathroom, or downstairs, looking for him. But he didn't believe either idea. She was sleeping too heavily when he left her.

He waited for a minute, listening, making up his mind what to do before it was too late. Then he went upstairs.

"Vicki?"

No reply. Andrew turned on the landing light. Something shot down the corridor. A mouse, or a spider. Nothing sinister.

"Vicki?"

Andrew was beginning to get spooked. The house

had swallowed up everybody but him. He tried to cling on to rational thought. It was the only tool he had left. Above him, he thought he heard a noise.

"Vicki?"

No sound. Why would she have gone up to the attic? Andrew could think of no reason, but there was no reason for her to have gone into any of the other rooms, either. He walked down the corridor, trying to remember where the entrance to the attic was concealed.

The first door he opened was Sandra's bedroom. The room had a foul, fetid smell, he noticed, which hadn't been there earlier. Everything else about the room was exactly as they had left it.

"Vicki?"

They'd forgotten to turn off the light, which Andrew did now. If the power ran out in the middle of the night, he'd never find Vicki. The next room he came to was the one he was looking for: a small servants' foyer with a door leading up to the attic. Or so Andrew thought. When he opened it, the passage led downwards, rather than up. He was confused, then remembered what Vicki had told him about the secret servants' passages which ran through the house. This one must lead down to McFadyen and Moira's rooms. The door at the bottom, locked this afternoon, was now ajar.

Andrew was about to open the opposite door, which must lead upwards, into the attic, when he heard a noise to his right, where there was no visible door. He pulled at the wooden panelling. It swung open and, sure enough, there was a concealed passage. Andrew poked his head into a narrow, unlit corridor. Someone was in there, holding a candle, which illuminated their face in a sickly, pale light. He couldn't make her out properly.

"Vicki?"

The figure shrieked, dropped the candle, and disappeared around a corner, but not until after Andrew had recognized her. It wasn't Vicki. It was her sister.

Sandra was gone before Andrew could register what was going on. He thought about following her, but the candle had gone out when it fell. He had no light. Sandra might know her way around these dark, narrow corridors, but Andrew didn't. And if Vicki's sister were still alive and living there, the chances were that she was responsible for at least some of what was going on in the house. Andrew already suspected her of having killed her mother. What if she had done the same to her father, sister and brother? It didn't bear thinking about.

Vicki had a torch in her room. Andrew went back down for it. If he was going to explore those dark, secret corridors again, he needed a light. He also needed a weapon. Having taken the torch from Vicki's dresser, Andrew hurried back down to the kitchen and looked for a sharp knife. His glass of milk was on the table where he'd left it earlier, empty. Andrew glanced at it, then opened a drawer, looking for something sharp.

He found table knives, forks, wooden spoons and three different whisks. In the next drawer he found a garlic press, a potato masher, two sieves and a rolling pin. Andrew was about to open the next drawer when he thought about the milk. He hadn't finished his glass of milk earlier. But someone had.

Andrew opened the next drawer. Tea towels. He looked at the wooden surfaces next to the cooker. There, to the left of the bread bin, was a wooden knife block. He walked casually to the bread bin and took a medium-sized knife from the middle of the block. He brushed his thumb against the blade, to make sure that it was sharp. Then, very slowly, he turned round. A figure stood in the shadows by the butler's pantry, a burnt-out candle by its side.

"Sandra?" Andrew murmured.

The figure didn't move. Knife in hand, Andrew stepped forward, whispering gently.

"I won't hurt you. Talk to me, please."

The figure cowered in the darkness. Andrew didn't dare move too quickly. She could rush back up the stairway she had come down and instantly lose him in the darkness. His torch was on the table. He was five metres away from her and didn't have time to grab it. Also, from the way she was hunched over, Sandra might easily be carrying some kind of weapon. But Andrew needed to get to her. He needed to find out what she'd done with Vicki.

"Please come here," he said. "I promise I won't hurt you." The figure half turned, getting ready to make a run for it.

"Don't leave," he pleaded. "Look. I'm moving away." Andrew took two steps to his side and the figure stopped moving.

"Let's talk," he said, taking another step to the right and reaching his hand out. He was hoping that he was groping in the right place. His hands fumbled along the wall. Then they hit the switch and another light came on.

The figure in the corner flinched. It wasn't hunched over, as Andrew had thought, and it wasn't Sandra.

It was Paul. His face, Andrew suddenly realized, was remarkably similar to his eldest sister's.

"Paul!" he said, heartily. "You scared me! I thought you were Sandra! Where've you been? Vicki and I have been worried about you."

"Upstairs," Paul said, in a quiet voice.

"We thought that you and your father had left."

"I hid in the attic." His small voice was trembling.

"Why?" Andrew said. "What's wrong? What are you afraid of?" The boy stared at Andrew, his timid, rabbit's eyes coming into focus as Andrew walked towards him.

"'Fraid of *you*."

Andrew stopped walking.

"Why?" he said. "What have I done to scare you?"

"Moira said."

"What did Moira say?"

Paul trembled.

"She told Daddy that he shouldn't trust you."

"Why did she say that?"

Andrew wanted to know what, if anything, Moira had against him. However, if Paul knew, he wasn't telling.

"Moira was wrong," Andrew said, softly. "You can trust me. I'd never do anything to hurt her, or you."

Paul didn't reply. His clothes, Andrew saw now, were filthy. His eyes were even more sunken and spaced out than they had been before.

"Do you know where Vicki is?" he asked, unable to hide some of the urgency in his voice.

Paul glanced up the stairway. He was thinking of making a run for it.

"Not telling," he said.

Andrew put the knife down and took another step towards Paul.

"Listen," he said in his kindest voice. "Moira's not here. I think that she and McFadyen left."

"Moira wouldn't do that. She wouldn't leave Vicki and me."

"OK," Andrew said. "Maybe you're right. But,

whatever's happened to her, she's not around. There's only you, me and Vicki. But I've lost Vicki. I need to find her. Do you know where she is?" Paul shook his head. Andrew tried another question.

"Do you know where Sandra is?"

He shook his head again.

"Why were you hiding in the attic?"

Paul didn't answer. Instead, he said:

"I'm hungry."

"I'll get you some food in a minute," Andrew promised, though he knew that there wasn't much of anything left. "What made you come downstairs again?"

"I heard something."

"What?"

"I heard Vicki, walking about beneath me, calling out."

"Why did you come down then? You didn't come when we called you earlier."

Paul's eyes narrowed.

"She wasn't calling me. She was calling you."

"I see. Then what happened?"

"I heard her open a door, close another. Then I heard her scream, and a banging noise. I was worried. I thought you'd hurt her."

The look on his face showed that he still suspected Andrew of having attacked his sister.

"When?" Andrew asked, urgently. "How long ago?"

"About five minutes before you came upstairs."

"Come on!" Andrew said, picking up the knife again. "We've got to find her."

"This way's quicker." Paul pointed up the dark staircase.

Andrew hurried after the boy, his torch ineffectually scattering its pale beam in Paul's wake. But Paul didn't need light, not even the candle he'd been holding before. He was, Andrew realized, used to moving about in the dark. They came out in the foyer which Andrew had entered a few minutes earlier.

"I think I know which one she might be in," he told Paul. They turned left. Why had Vicki screamed? If Andrew hadn't been so far down, in the kitchen, he would have heard her too. If anything had happened to Vicki, he would never forgive himself.

"Which room?" Paul asked.

"Sandra's bedroom," Andrew guessed. "There was a light on in there earlier which shouldn't have been. Come on."

They went into the bedroom where he'd turned off the light a few minutes before. But, this time, Andrew noticed another light, seeping out of the dressing-room. He switched on the main light and saw that the dressing-room door was ajar. He was about to go in there when something stopped him.

A bloodstained arm pushed the door fully open.

Vicki staggered into the bedroom, pale as a ghost. One side of her nightdress was speckled with blood. Andrew rushed to her arms.

"You're bleeding!"

"It … it's all right," Vicki stuttered. "It's not my blood."

"What happened?"

"A noise woke me up and you weren't there. I called your name. Then I thought I heard something moving about upstairs. I … I guessed you couldn't sleep. I thought you must have decided to finish searching the house. But I didn't want to be alone, so I came up after you."

"I should never have left you," Andrew told her. "I'm sorry."

"Someone was moving about upstairs," Vicki repeated. Her voice was a dazed monotone. She seemed to be suffering from shock.

"It was Paul."

"I came into this room. I remembered this was the last room we came to before the power failed. The bedroom light wasn't on, but the dressing-room light was. I thought you might be in there, so I went in and … and…"

"What?"

"There was one wardrobe door, half open."

"What? What?"

Vicki stared at him helplessly.

"Don't let Paul see it."

Andrew let go of her. Paul came over, sheepishly. Brother and sister held hands. Andrew opened the dressing-room door again and looked to his right, at the wardrobe. He'd been about to check it when the lights went out in the storm: the wardrobe with the sweet, sickly smell. There, hanging in the middle, was a bloodstained wedding dress. Vicki's sister Sandra was wearing it, with a dagger twisted into her heart. Judging by the smell coming from her, she had been dead for days.

18

Back in the bedroom, Paul and Vicki stood exactly where he'd left them.

"Come on," Andrew said. "Let's go downstairs."

Vicki began to cough. Andrew didn't know whether she'd told Paul what had happened to his elder sister, and he didn't ask.

"I'm cold," Paul said.

Andrew turned off the lights behind them.

"We're nearly out of fuel for the generator," he told Paul. "We have to conserve power."

"There might be some wood in Daddy's bedroom," Vicki said, in her half-asleep voice. "We could go there."

"Good idea."

While Andrew made the fire, Vicki talked to Paul.

He told her what he'd told Andrew earlier, but in more detail.

"You don't know where Daddy's gone?" she asked when he'd finished.

"No."

"He didn't say anything about going away?"

"No."

"Do you know if Daddy ever found Sandra?"

"I don't think so."

"And what about you, Paul. Did you see Sandra?"

He shook his head.

"Is she? Is she?"

"Like Mummy. I'm afraid so."

As the fire flickered into life, Paul burst into tears.

"I never wanted any of this to happen. Never!"

Vicki cuddled him.

"'Course you didn't. No one did."

She was wrong, Andrew knew. Someone had wanted Sandra and her mother dead. Someone very close to home.

As brother and sister huddled in front of the fire, Andrew tried to work out what was going on. The main suspect for Lady Hetherington's death, Sandra, had been murdered herself. That left four more people who had both means and motive to murder mother and daughter: Vicki's father, McFadyen, Moira and Paul.

Or maybe it should be five. Vicki could have

caused the accident, could have killed her sister, too, but it seemed highly unlikely. She'd only been back in the house for a day when her mother died. As for Sandra, there were times when Vicki could have stabbed her, but Sandra was bigger and stronger than Vicki was. Whoever had put Sandra in that wedding dress, then hung her in the wardrobe like a slab of meat, was either a strong person, or had an accomplice. No. Not Vicki. Andrew might as well suspect Alice, all those miles away on her family farm.

Could Lord Hetherington have killed his wife? He was out of the country at the time. Or so he had led them to believe. When Vicki phoned him in South Africa, he had already left. However, Andrew doubted that he was strong enough to do what had been done to Sandra, either. Which left the two servants. Andrew was inclined to discount Moira. She had been with the family nearly twenty years, and was clearly loyal to them. He was beginning to worry about what had happened to her. Both Paul and Vicki felt that she wouldn't walk out on them. In which case...

That only left McFadyen. Andrew knew little about the butler. He was quiet, and seemingly efficient, despite a shortage of staff to help him. Andrew had assumed that he walked out for the same reason as Alice – not being paid. But maybe the butler wasn't all he seemed. Andrew decided to talk it over with Vicki.

"I've been thinking…"

"Ssssh…" Vicki pointed at Paul, who had nodded off to sleep. "Help me put him in Daddy's bed. Then we'll talk."

They carefully laid Paul in his father's double bed, dirty clothes and all. Then they sat down by the fire.

"What do we do next?" Andrew asked, in a low voice.

"I reckon that, first thing in the morning, we get out of here. As soon as it's light, walk to the nearest place with a phone, and call the police."

"Sounds sensible to me," Andrew said. "Who do you think did it?"

"I don't know," Vicki told him. "I've been thinking about Mummy – maybe her death wasn't an accident. Do you think that Sandra could have killed Mummy, then stabbed herself?"

"Hanging from the coat rail like that? I don't think so."

"In that case," Vicki said, "it could be anyone: an escaped lunatic, a serial killer."

Andrew yawned. It had been a very long day. Fear and adrenalin had kept him going, but now he was exhausted.

"I can't see an escaped lunatic serial killer coming all the way to the Cheviots, can you? Whoever it is, I think we'll find the solution in this house. This isn't random. This is connected to the history of the Hetherington family. I'm sure of it."

Vicki was silent.

"Any ideas?" Andrew asked.

"I'll think about it," Vicki assured him. "Let's talk about it in the morning, when we're both more awake."

Andrew was too tired to take it any further.

"Listen," Vicki went on. "I think that one of us should stay awake all the time, just in case. I've had more sleep than you, so I'll do the first shift. You get down near the fire and I'll do until three. You can do three till five, then I'll keep watch until daybreak. OK?"

"OK."

The fire was warm and the heat from it began to cloud Andrew's head. He quickly fell asleep. At three, Vicki woke him and he did the next two hours in a sleepy haze. Nothing happened. Then Vicki did another turn. When Andrew woke again at seven, she was sat on the hearthrug, staring blankly at the fire's embers. Paul slept on. Vicki and Andrew hugged.

"What's that noise?" Vicki said, breaking away. It was coming from outside the house. He snapped fully awake.

"Sounds like an engine."

"Please, let it be the police," Vicki said.

They went to the window. Through the dirty

glass, Andrew could make out something red, parking outside the front door.

"It's the post," he said.

"I forgot about the post," Vicki said. "Brilliant! We can get a lift to the phone. Come on."

Andrew tried to open the window and call out.

"It's stuck."

"It's always been stuck. Come downstairs. Quickly."

As Paul blinked awake, Vicki and Andrew hurried down to the ground floor. Two envelopes lay on the mat in the hall. Andrew kicked them aside as Vicki fumbled with the lock on the front door. Then she pulled it open. As they rushed out into the damp, overcast day, Vicki still in her blood-splattered nightdress, they saw the Post Office van turning round in the drive.

"Hey!" Vicki yelled. "Wait!"

The van finished turning and slowly set off.

"Wait!" they both shouted.

Vicki and Andrew began to run up the drive. Surely the driver could hear them? But the van was old and its engine noisy.

"Wait!"

As they got closer to it, the van began to accelerate. They ran after it for a long time, waving their arms madly. All it would take was for the driver to look once into her rear view mirror. But it didn't happen. The van disappeared into the distance.

Disappointed, the couple walked back to the Hall. It began to drizzle.

"We'll have to walk it later on," Vicki said.

Andrew agreed. The rain became heavier. When they got back to the Hall, the front door still hung open. It was scarcely any warmer inside than it was out.

"You'd better get dressed," Andrew said to Vicki. "Is there any more wood around that I could collect for a fire?"

"You could start smashing up the furniture," she said. He wasn't sure if she was being serious.

Andrew picked up the mail from the floor and handed it to Vicki. One letter was addressed to Vicki, airmail from Israel, and she tucked it into the pocket of her nightgown. The other was for her father. It was postmarked Kelso, the previous day.

"I think it's from Mr Gallagher," Vicki said. "I'd better open it."

She was right. The name at the top of the heavy, cream paper was "C. Gallagher, Solicitor." The letter read as follows:

My Lord,

I have, in accordance with your wishes, prepared the contracts and deed of sale, transferring ownership of Hetherington Hall to Mr Brickell. Mr Brickell's solicitor informs me that the deposit is ready for transfer.

You may recall that we had an appointment at four this afternoon for you to sign the contract and endorse any alterations which you have decided to make to your will. When you did not arrive, I telephoned the Hall repeatedly, but could not get through. British Telecom inform me that there appears to be a fault on the line, but they cannot deal with it until you complain in person.

I have received several faxes from Mr Brickell's solicitors wishing to confirm our exchange of contracts. I would be grateful if you would contact me and arrange a fresh appointment to deal with these matters as quickly as possible. I would, of course, be willing to come to the Hall if you are indisposed.

I have the honour to remain,
> *My Lord,*
>> *Your Lordship's obedient servant,*
>> *Charles Gallagher.*

Vicki put the letter down.

"So Daddy meant to go straight from our family meeting to signing the contracts which sold off the Hall."

"It looks like it," Andrew replied. "But he didn't get there. Why?"

"That," said Vicki, "is something I'd really like to know."

"You don't think that someone here might…"

Vicki's voice became angry.

"If I'd known that Daddy was about to sell off the house," she said, "I might even have killed him myself."

"Don't talk like that," Andrew said. "Let's try the phone."

"To get the police?"

"Yes. But I'd like to talk to Gallagher first. It seems to me that he might be the one person who knows what's going on."

But the phone was still dead.

Paul, Vicki and Andrew dressed, then ate breakfast in the kitchen. They had stale muesli soaked in long-life orange juice, washed down by tea made with powdered milk, the remaining dairy milk having gone sour. While they ate, Vicki read her letter from Israel.

"Interesting?" Andrew asked, surprised that she could do something so normal as read a letter.

"Just kibbutz gossip. I'm not really taking it in."

Andrew stared into space, thinking. He was fairly sure now that Lord Hetherington was dead. He expected that Vicki had worked this out, too, but didn't discuss it with her. He was no nearer to working out who had killed Lord Hetherington's wife and eldest daughter, or why.

When they'd eaten, they went up to the hall and tried the phone again. No change. Andrew decided to question Paul some more before they went.

"Is there anything you've seen in the house while you were hiding, Paul? Anyone in places where they shouldn't be?"

The boy shook his head apathetically. Andrew pressed him.

"Think, *please*. You spent all that time up in the attic. Who came up to see you? Who was on the second floor apart from Sandra?"

Paul spoke slowly.

"Daddy came to see me."

"What about the servants: Moira, McFadyen?"

"No."

Andrew dredged his mind for other ideas.

"How about someone who used to work here? Alice, for instance?"

"No."

"This is getting us nowhere," Vicki said. "The rain's over. Let's go."

Andrew was stubborn.

"I wonder whether we should search the house one more time before we leave," he suggested. "We haven't looked through all of the servants' passages you told me about, or the cellar. We might find..."

"No," Vicki asserted, bluntly. "We'll leave that to the police. I want to get Paul out of here. I want to get out of here myself."

Andrew had to admit she had a point.

"All right," he said.

"Paul, go and get your coat."

"He knows something," Andrew told Vicki when Paul was out of the room. "Why did he hide away in the attic like that? It doesn't make sense. He knows something he's not telling us."

"Maybe," Vicki said, in a pointed voice, avoiding Andrew's gaze. "It's pretty hard to know what goes on in other people's minds, isn't it?"

She gave Andrew a hard, peculiar look. He judged it best not to ask what she meant by her remark.

19

Outside, the sky was still dark and threatened to rain again. They took the route which Vicki and Andrew had travelled the day before, but in reverse. Alice's farm was, it seemed, the nearest occupied building with a phone.

The three of them moved more slowly than the day before. Paul was small for his age and found it hard to keep up. Both he and Vicki seemed preoccupied and didn't talk. Andrew tried to take his mind back through the events of the last few days, looking for loose ends which might mean something. Could the South African who was buying the house be behind the deaths? What did Doctor Rutherford want with Lord Hetherington? Could McFadyen or Moira have a motive for the murders?

He came up with no answers at all.

"We ought to go this way," Paul said, when they came to two paths at the end of a field. "It's quicker."

"I prefer this one," Vicki said.

"Why?" Paul moaned. "I thought you said we were in a hurry."

"What is it?" Andrew asked, gently. "Why can't we go the way that Paul suggests?"

"Oh, very well," Vicki agreed, reluctantly.

The path came up through woods, then led down again, into a valley. They crossed a drystone wall in a bad state of disrepair.

"Are we still in Hetherington land?" Andrew asked Vicki.

"I don't think so."

Then Andrew saw what Vicki had wanted to avoid. They were in a valley. Ahead of them, a track snaked through the hills. Before them were the ruins of a big house. Only the low outline of its ground floor was still standing.

"Partington House?" Andrew asked Vicki.

She nodded.

"Have you been here before?" he asked Paul.

"It's a great place to play. Look!"

"Not now, Paul."

Ignoring his sister, Paul hurried on towards the house. Andrew found his behaviour bizarre. He was acting like a child on holiday.

"I'd better go after him," Andrew said. He followed Paul into the ruin, while Vicki trudged on towards the track ahead.

Partington House had once been the size of Hetherington Hall, or bigger. The little of it left standing gave the impression that it was a more airy, less claustrophobic building. In the middle of it, Andrew walked through what was once one of the main rooms. Then his foot slipped.

Andrew grabbed on to the wall and levered his foot out from where it was trapped. He'd mildly twisted his ankle, but realized that he'd been in danger of much worse. Below Andrew was the cellar. In places, the floorboard had been burnt away, or collapsed. Here, grass had grown over it, but the boards beneath were loose and rotten, decayed by fire and ten years of hard Northumberland weather. If they had given way, he could have had a nasty fall.

"This place is a deathtrap," he told Paul. "They should put up notices."

"No one ever comes here," Paul replied. "Except me, and I'm not meant to. But I know the safe way round. You should follow me more closely. Come on, I'll show you the best bit."

"Let's just get out of here," Andrew protested, but Paul was on his way.

Gingerly, because he was two or three times Paul's weight, Andrew followed Paul along one of the main foundation walls, then round a corner where he could make out what was once a big window, looking out on to the wood behind.

"Very nice," he told Paul. "But now we'd better catch Vicki up."

"Look at this first."

Paul charged on. It was odd, the way he was behaving, like a little boy playing games. He was, Andrew decided, too young to really take in the deaths of his sister and mother. Paul wanted to show Andrew this place that he loved, failing to realize that several people must have died in the fire here. Andrew humoured him.

"Where are you, Paul? I've lost you."

"Over here."

He was two rooms away, at the edge of the house.

"Is it safe?"

"Just go straight ahead."

Andrew did as he suggested. Gorse was growing through the floorboards. He dodged the prickliest sections. In the distance, he could see Vicki, walking up the hill. Then he looked around and could no longer see Paul.

"Paul!"

The boy was behind him.

"Sorry, Andy," Paul said, pushing him. "She told me to."

Before Andrew knew what was happening, he lost his balance. Paul pushed him harder. Andrew was suddenly terrified. The ground beneath him was anything but safe. He was falling into a black hole.

He grabbed at the gorse. It tore his hands, and began to come away. His body slammed against one of the cellar's side walls. As the gorse gave way, he slid down the wall.

Andrew landed with a thud. If he had fallen straight down, in the middle of the cellar, he would have been killed, or done himself a severe injury. As it was, all he got was a mighty jolt. He had cut his hand. His skin was cut, bruised and scraped in several places.

What had Paul meant to do? Andrew tried to piece together the meaning of his last words. *She told me to*. He could only be referring to Vicki or Moira. Why would Vicki wish such an accident on him? She had, Andrew remembered, been behaving strangely. Alice's words about the "mad sisters" echoed in his brain. Yet, even if Vicki was unbalanced in some way, why had she chosen to have Paul attack him, now? Nothing added up.

The cellar was very dark and cold, but Andrew was in no hurry to get out of it. He was in a quandary. Should he go after Vicki, and attempt to protect her? Or should he lie low, letting Vicki and Paul think that he'd been knocked out, or worse? He no longer knew if he should be trying to protect his girlfriend or hiding from her.

Andrew moved slowly, partly because of his

bruises and partly because he didn't want to attract attention from above. He had to find the cellar steps. He prayed that they were made of stone. For, if they were wood, and had been burnt away in the fire ten years ago, he could be trapped here for ever.

Andrew felt his way along the walls. There was the odd glint of light from above, but barely enough to see by. He might have passed the steps, for all he knew. There could be any kind of trap waiting for him. He remembered how, the last time he was in the cellars of Hetherington Hall, he'd thought he heard someone screaming. This time, the person screaming would be him.

Andrew edged his way along. Something moved under his feet and, for a horrible moment, he thought that the ground was going to give way beneath him again. But it was only a lizard, darting out of danger. Andrew stumbled on, realizing that he had no sense of geography. Which way to go? At one end of the ruined house, the cellar was completely exposed. There would be light. He could see, but he could be seen from above, too. The question was: seen by who?

It didn't make sense. If Vicki wanted to kill him, why would she get Paul to do it? If the deaths were all to do with the Hetherington inheritance, Vicki had nothing to gain by Andrew's death. Unless she thought that he... Another idea occurred to Andrew. Maybe Vicki's behaviour today was connected to the letter that morning – not the one to her father, but the other one, to her, from Israel. What was in it?

Andrew decided that he had to chance it. He had to get out of the cellar and go to her. For, if Vicki was innocent, she must be in enormous danger.

Andrew was distracted by a noise: a gentle moan, or whimper. There was someone else in this section of the cellar with him. Where? Andrew didn't know whether to run from the noise or go to it. He saw a gap in the floorboards over to the side of him. A small shaft of light poked through it. Cautiously, Andrew made his way to where the noise was coming from, using the light to guide him. Whoever it was, they might need help.

The noise stopped. Andrew stumbled on. There was a louder moan as he nearly fell over a body. Pulling himself upright, Andrew could make him out: face sunken, one eye open, more dead than alive. It was Vicki's father.

"What happened to you?" Andrew asked. "How did you get here?"

Lord Hetherington gasped for words. Close up, his lungs sounded bad. His breathing was shallow and raspy.

"She ... lured ... me ... here," he said. "Y-yesterday."

"Who?"

"Broke ... both ... my ... legs."

159

He opened his eyes briefly, and managed two full sentences.

"I … know who … you are. It's … up to … you, now."

"I'll help you," Andrew said. "I'll go for help. Just tell me who did this. Please."

Lord Hetherington's eyes were closed. Andrew could tell that he was fading fast. He had only just got here in time.

"Please, Lord Hetherington. Stay awake a moment longer, please. Tell me who brought you here."

His mouth opened and closed.

"My … daugh … ter."

"Vicki? Do you mean that Vicki's behind this?"

The sound he made next was merely a whisper, and Andrew wasn't even sure that he'd heard it.

"Sh…"

"What? Please tell me. I don't understand."

The mouth opened and closed again.

"…"

Andrew took Lord Hetherington's pulse. He was dead.

20

Before leaving Lord Hetherington, Andrew searched his pockets. He took his wallet from a trouser pocket and a large manila envelope from the breast pocket of his jacket, then put them into his borrowed Barbour. He also found a cigarette lighter, and used it to make his way to the stairs which, thankfully, were made of stone. Andrew clambered safely into daylight just as it began to rain.

There was no sign of Paul or Vicki, for which Andrew was grateful. Which way to go? He hadn't come by this route before. He might easily overshoot Alice's farm, and there wasn't another dwelling for miles. The wind was getting up and the rain was becoming stronger. Not only that, but he'd twisted his ankle earlier and the fall into the cellar had badly shaken him up. There was no way he could walk for miles and miles in this condition, even if he knew the route to Alice's farm. There was only one thing for it. He would have to make the short walk back to Hetherington Hall.

Andrew calculated that he had a small advantage. No one knew that he was alive. He would probably have the house to himself, at least until the police came. That was, presuming Vicki and Paul went for the police. What story would they tell? That their sister was dead and their father had vanished? Perhaps they would blame Andrew for the murders. Perhaps the whole thing had been planned from the start. Vicki had lured Andrew to the Hall in order to make him the scapegoat. It was a frightening thought.

By the time Andrew reached Hetherington Hall, he was soaked and, though it was only early afternoon, the sky was dark as night. There were no lights on in the building. It was almost certainly empty. But Andrew took no chances, going in by the back door, next to the garage. The stable doors, he noticed, had been closed. He didn't remember Vicki doing that.

Which room to go into? Safest, he thought, to choose one where the light would not be seen from outside the house. Andrew went to Lord Hetherington's study, treading quietly in case Paul or Vicki had returned. Once inside the study, he put on the desk lamp, adjusting the light carefully so that it couldn't be seen through the bottom of the door. Keeping his Barbour on, for the house was very cold, he took out Lord Hetherington's wallet and the large brown envelope.

Before he could open them, Andrew heard someone coming in through the front door. Hurriedly, he stuffed the envelope and wallet back into his pockets. To be on the safe side, he turned out the desk lamp. Then he heard two sets of footsteps, coming towards him. It sounded like Vicki and Paul. Andrew stood behind the door in case one of them came into the room.

But the people weren't coming towards him. They were going upstairs. Cautiously, Andrew slid the door open. It was too late to see anything, but he heard part of a conversation.

"...can't have got far. She's probably sheltering somewhere, or looking for her precious boyfriend. We'll wait till the rain stops, then go out for her again in the car."

"Why did you try to run her over?" Paul asked.

"I explained," the voice said. "She pretends to be your friend, but she isn't. You won't be safe while she's around." Andrew trembled. Although the woman's voice was familiar, he couldn't work out who it belonged to. It was a Hetherington voice, yet it wasn't Vicki's. Then the voice became more tender.

"Are you all right? Can you go through with this?"

"Yes," Paul's voice replied.

"You're sure?"

"I'm sure, Mummy."

Then they were out of earshot. Andrew was dumbfounded. He had seen Lady Hetherington's body in the bath. He had been at her funeral. Yet ... right now, he was prepared to believe anything. Had Lady Hetherington somehow faked her own death, in order to take revenge on the family who didn't love her?

Andrew sneaked upstairs, not by the main staircase, but by the servants' one. He now had a pretty good idea of how the hidden passages in the house worked. However, when he peeked out on the first floor, there was no sign of Paul or his "mother". It was deadly quiet.

Andrew was about to go up to the second floor when he heard a door open. He snatched a look down the corridor, then quickly withdrew his head. They were coming towards him. Both were in shadows, so Andrew couldn't properly see the woman with Paul. She could be anyone. But he could see which room they'd come from. It was Vicki's.

The woman's voice was saying:

"I knew it, I knew it! I thought he came to marry her, but it was more than that! He came for revenge, Paul! Moira was right." Paul's small voice came next.

"I liked him. He was nice to me. I didn't want to…"

"You have to be strong, Paul. We'll go back later, make sure he's dead. When we call the police, I don't want them to find their murderer still alive and denying everything."

"What about Vicki?" Paul asked.

"She's probably back there, looking for him."

"Even after she got that letter?"

There was a pause before the woman spoke again.

"Maybe you're right. But Vicki doesn't know the full story, so I doubt that she's ready to desert him yet. Now, before we look for her, can you reconnect the phone? I need to call Doctor Rutherford."

"I'll do it now, Mummy," Paul said.

Paul went downstairs, while his companion went up. As Andrew came out into the corridor, he could hear Paul going into the cellar. It had been him all along, disconnecting the phones whenever he was told to. Before Andrew found out anything else, he wanted to know what was in the letter which Vicki received that morning. As quietly as he could, Andrew made his way to her room.

The letter lay open on her desk. It was from one of Vicki's friends, Freya. She was taking a year out in Israel, on a kibbutz. The letter began by thanking Vicki for her postcard from Greece.

Glad you're having a great time. Can't wait to meet

your new guy. I wish you'd told me more about him. Is he from Bretton or did you meet him on holiday? What does he look like? What does he do?

Then there was a load of stuff about the kibbutz and Freya's sex life, which Andrew skipped. Before he knew it, the letter was over. Andrew was mystified as to what had had such a big effect on Vicki. Then he turned the last page over and found a PS.

By the way, I meant to tell you at the end of term, but never found you. You were probably working on your exhibit for the Summer Show. Thing is, there was this guy at Bretton, asking lots of questions about you: where were you from, who were your family, what kinds of things did you like, did you have a boyfriend, all that kind of stuff. He was very good looking: tall, thin, brown curly hair – your type, really – but there was something a bit creepy about the way he was acting. I didn't tell him much. His name was Andrew something. If I were you, I'd watch out for him when you go back.

Andrew put the letter down. It could have been worse. All it meant was that Vicki knew that they hadn't bumped into each other by accident at the Henry Moore exhibition in June. Andrew had known that Vicki often visited the sculptures, and used them to get the opportunity to strike up a conversation with her. He could understand her being upset when she discovered this deception. But he had his reasons. She would see that. He could explain it to her.

Andrew had to get to Vicki before Paul and the woman he called "Mummy" did. Would Vicki still trust Andrew? She had to give him the benefit of the doubt. Earlier, he'd heard "Mummy" talk about going out in the car. She must have been using the Bentley, "borrowing" it from Lord Hetherington after his fall. Andrew needed the car. Vicki, he remembered, had picked up the spare set of keys earlier. Where would she have put them? He looked around her room, praying that she hadn't taken them with her.

Andrew didn't have far to look. The keys were amongst the mess of stuff on Vicki's desk. He picked them up and edged back into the corridor. He had to get out to the back door without being seen. This meant that he had to go down the main staircase. Andrew didn't know where Paul was. He prayed that he wouldn't bump into him as he sneaked out of Hetherington Hall.

Andrew crept down the stairs. Every creak sounded like a death threat, yet no one came. He got to the main hall and was half-way to the back door when the place seemed to explode.

Andrew nearly jumped out of his skin, but it was only the phone ringing. Heavy feet hurried down the stairs. At first, Andrew was going to hide in Lord Hetherington's study, but there was a phone in there, too. So, instead, Andrew ducked into the breakfast room, where he could just make out the telephone table by the staircase.

The phone kept ringing. Andrew hoped that it wouldn't stop before whoever it was got there. It didn't. From the breakfast room, Andrew saw a slim arm reach out to pick the receiver up. When Andrew saw the arm's owner, his heart nearly stopped. He was looking at a dead woman.

It was Sandra.

21

She had lost a little weight, it seemed. From where Andrew was standing, Sandra looked more like her neurotic mother than a body builder. He guessed that this was because she had been starving herself, hiding out in the house's attics and secret passageways for days. Maybe it was her whom he had seen in the passage yesterday, not Paul. Her voice sounded different, too. Not like when he'd first met her, nor like the voice he'd heard that afternoon. Sandra seemed to be putting on a kind of forced jollity for the telephone.

"Doctor Rutherford. I was about to call you myself. Yes, the phone has been out of order. BT have only just repaired it. My father wanted to get back to you, but he's not been well. I see … yes. No,

I'm Sandra, her sister … I'm afraid he can't come to the phone. He's still ill. You know that my mother died last week? We're all terribly upset. If you could be brief…"

There was a long pause while Sandra listened. Then she spoke again.

"No. Not at all. No contact since … it happened. The family completely cut her off. The baby was adopted. I don't know the details. She wouldn't be able to trace … no, good, of course not. I expect that she'll want to start a new life, a long way away. It was good of you to call us, though. I'll tell my father what you've told me… There's no need to get in touch again. We can contact you if anything comes up. All right. Thank you. Goodbye."

She put the phone down. As Andrew watched, a look of triumph spread across her face. She said "*yes*" to herself in a kind of hiss. Then she walked quickly back up the stairs, skipping every other step.

Andrew got out of the house as quickly as he could. He opened the garage doors to find that he was right: the Bentley had been returned. He got into it and examined the controls, praying that he could get the car to work. He had to find Vicki before Sandra did.

The Bentley started first time. Luckily, the car was an automatic and easy to operate. The engine purred as Andrew drove out of the garage, on to the long driveway, hoping that whatever Sandra and

Paul were doing inside was noisy enough for them not to hear him leave.

It seemed an age before he was out of sight of the house, but it was probably only a minute. Which way to go? Andrew tried to remember the way to Alice's farm, where there was a phone, but knew he'd get lost on the winding minor roads. His best hope was to make it to Partington House, which was where he'd last seen Vicki. Where was she? And if she saw the car, what would she think? Did she know that Sandra was still alive, and probably wanted to kill her?

How come Sandra was alive? Andrew thought about the body in the wardrobe. It looked real, and smelt disgusting. But neither he, nor Vicki, had examined it closely. And Paul, who didn't look at it, hardly seemed shocked at all. Maybe he knew it was a mannequin, smeared with real blood – say, from an animal, whose carcass had been left in the wardrobe to create a convincing smell. Yes, that made sense. But why would Paul and Sandra put it there?

Maybe the faked death wasn't aimed at Vicki, but at Sandra's father. Lord Hetherington had a weak heart. Sandra must have known that he would go looking for his eldest daughter eventually. When he found the mannequin in the wardrobe, she hoped that he would do more than faint – he would have a heart attack, and die.

But what would be the point of killing him? And why did Paul call Sandra "Mummy"?

Of course. Everything made sense if Sandra really *was* Paul's mother. Lady Hetherington was younger than her husband, but not substantially so. She was in her early to mid-fifties when she died. She would have been at least forty-three when Paul was born. That wasn't an impossible age to have a child, especially these days, but it was still pretty late in life.

Sandra, on the other hand, would have been nineteen or twenty when Paul was born. She was due to have married, but it was called off. Suppose that part of the reason for her deep distress was that she was already pregnant? Suppose Paul was her son, by Charles Partington. That would make Paul...

Andrew stopped himself from jumping to conclusions and tried to recall the details of the phone call he'd overheard between Sandra and Dr Mary Rutherford. Adoption had been discussed then. Sandra said something about there being no contact, but she talked about the mother in the third person, about her wanting to start a new life. He couldn't figure it out.

Yet if Sandra were Paul's mother, it would explain the strong resemblance between them. And Vicki had told him, more than once, that Lord Hetherington had always wanted a son. So, of course, he and Lady Hetherington would have adopted Paul. But could an adopted son inherit a title? Andrew didn't know.

Absorbed in these questions, Andrew nearly missed the turning which would take him in the direction of Partington House. He prayed that Vicki was still somewhere nearby. A few cows grazed to his right. There was no sign of Vicki.

Andrew took a turning and found himself on the narrow track which went round a hill, then down into the valley which contained the ruins of Partington House. As he passed the brow of the hill he saw someone. Vicki was walking slowly along a footpath not far from the road. He'd found her.

Andrew braked sharply. Before he could get out of the car, Vicki ran off, over the fields. Andrew got out of the car and ran after her, yelling.

"Vicki, wait! Vicki, I've come to help you. Stop."

But it did no good. She just ran all the faster, towards the ruined house, where four people had already died for no good reason that Andrew knew of. He didn't want Vicki to be the fifth.

Andrew followed. His body was bruised and battered from the fall earlier, but Vicki, too, seemed tired. He began to catch her up. At least, he thought, she could hear what he was calling.

"Vicki, don't go into the ruins. They're dangerous."

But his words seemed to have the opposite effect.

Vicki ran straight into the shell of Partington House, towards the very area where Andrew had fallen earlier.

"Vicki, stop! You'll fall!"

Too late. One moment, she was there. The next, she was gone. Andrew reached the edge of the house himself, but couldn't see her.

He had to go after her. Cautiously clinging to the remains of the walls, he edged his way around the ruin, searching for her.

"Vicki, where are you?"

She didn't answer. Then, for a moment, the wind dropped, and Andrew could hear her anxious breathing, her involuntary whimpering, only feet away from him.

"Vicki, it's all right. I'll help you."

Her voice, when she spoke, was bitter and full of recriminations.

"Stay away from me!"

"I've never done anything to hurt you, Vicki."

"I'll jump!"

"Don't. You could kill yourself."

"Why do you care? You've already tried to kill me once today."

"What do you mean? How?"

"In the Bentley. You tried to run me over."

"Just now? I didn't see you. I wasn't trying to..."

"No. Earlier. When I was walking to Alice's and you and Paul deserted me."

Andrew saw that Vicki was clinging to a piece of wall. As she spoke to him, she was trying to pull herself up, but her efforts were having the opposite effect to the one she intended. The ground around her was falling away, and the stones in the wall were working loose.

"Vicki, you have to believe this: it wasn't me in the Bentley earlier. I was trapped in the cellar that you're about to fall into. Let me help you."

"No."

"Vicki, your father's already down there. He's dead. Please let me help you."

"Daddy? No. I don't believe ... no, get off!"

As Andrew was speaking, he'd got nearer to her, and now he grabbed Vicki's arm, pulling her out.

"Let me help! You can kill yourself later if you want!" The bit of wall which Andrew was holding on to gave way.

They both fell head first into the darkness.

22

Andrew came round to the taste of Vicki's lips against his.

"Please wake up, Andrew, please."

"I am awake," he mumbled.

"I guess," she said, as his eyes blinked open and she came into focus, "this means that you really do love me."

Andrew's mind was hazy. He had no idea how long he'd been unconscious.

"Why? What did I do?"

"You tried to stop me falling and nearly killed yourself. You broke my fall. Are you all right? Can you stand up?"

"Sure I'm all right. My head aches. That's all."

She helped him to his feet. It wasn't just his head,

Andrew realized. Everything ached.

"How long was I out for?"

"Ten, fifteen minutes," Vicki said. "You don't look too good to me. Do you think we can get out of here?"

"No problem," he assured her. "I've already done it once today."

They moved away from the hole they'd fallen through and the little light it cast, into blackness.

"It's awfully dark," Vicki said.

Andrew reached into his pocket.

"*Voilà!*"

Vicki gripped his hand.

"That's Daddy's lighter."

"I'm afraid so."

"Is what you said earlier true? Is he…?"

"Yes." Andrew kept talking to Vicki as she cried. "He told me that his daughter lured him here. I thought that he meant you, but actually, he meant Sandra."

"Sandra's dead!" Vicki exclaimed.

"She isn't. I've seen her."

"And I've seen her body. Where's Daddy?"

"Over there."

Vicki took the lighter and sat quietly with her father. Andrew watched as she said a prayer over his limp body.

"I took something from his pocket," Andrew said, after a while. "I think it's the will."

Vicki nodded and stood up.

"We'd better get out of here," Andrew said. "Paul and Sandra will come looking for us. They want to kill both of us."

"Why?"

"I don't know," he said. "Maybe Sandra wants to inherit the house, the money…"

Vicki joined him.

"Another thing," Andrew said, as they walked towards the steps.

"What?"

"From what I heard Paul and Sandra saying, I don't think that your mother was Paul's mother. I think that Sandra was. It explains a lot."

Andrew couldn't see Vicki's expression, but her voice was full of disdain.

"It might explain a lot," Vicki said, "but it isn't true. I was with Sandra when Mummy went away to have the baby. Sandra wasn't pregnant. She was depressed, manic even. But not pregnant."

"If it's not Sandra, then who…?"

"I was beginning to think that you were the person behind all this. The letter I got from Freya this morning freaked me out."

They emerged into the overcast day. The rain had stopped, but it was hard to tell, because the trees, heavy with water, were letting it fall in a soft, steady flow of droplets. Vicki looked at Andrew with a sceptical, weary face.

"Who *are* you?" she asked.

It was time to tell her everything.

23

"Andrew Wakefield's my real name. The aunt, the one I told you about, she adopted me. Wakefield's her ex-husband's name."

"I thought you didn't get on with her."

"I didn't. They sent me away to schools. When I came home in the holidays, we argued so much that I begged to leave. I ended up boarding full-time from when I was thirteen. I haven't seen them for years."

"And your real parents. Who were they?"

Andrew hesitated.

"You've probably worked that out already."

"The Partingtons?"

He nodded.

"I was away at school when the house burnt

down. I haven't been back since. They wouldn't let me go to the funeral. My aunt never told me how it really happened. She made up a story about a car crash – because she thought it would be less upsetting, I guess – but I always knew that there was something mysterious which I hadn't been told.

"You know, I looked through the microfiche at college, and it wasn't even in the papers. Now and then, I'd hear my aunt talking about what happened when I wasn't meant to be listening. They used your family's name. Then, when I went to Bretton, I heard someone mention you. I asked people about you. When I found out where you were from, I knew that I had to get to know you, to find out what happened to my family."

"And have you found out?" Vicki asked.

Andrew shook his head.

"Not completely. I know that Sandra was supposed to marry my older brother, Charles. He'd graduated from university the summer before the fire. But I don't know what happened then. Did he jilt Sandra? Or did he die in the fire before the marriage could take place?"

Andrew looked back at the ruin.

"It must have been quite a fire, to destroy the building so badly. The entire side section is missing."

"That's where they kept the oil tank and the generator," Vicki explained.

"Aah."

Vicki stood on the edge of the ruins, thinking.

"We must have met," she said, "when we were children."

"Yes."

"Why did you lie to me?" she asked. "Why couldn't you have been honest?"

"Would you have told me the truth?"

Vicki looked away.

"I don't know," she said. "But if I'd known who you were, I wouldn't have allowed myself to fall in love with you."

"I fell in love with you, too," Andrew said. "It wasn't part of a plan."

Now Vicki turned to him. This wasn't the time to talk about love.

"Are you sure Daddy said that Sandra lured him here?"

Andrew tried to recollect Lord Hetherington's final words precisely.

"He said 'my daughter'. At the time, I thought he was talking about you. I asked him again. The last thing he said sounded like 'Sh…' I assumed he was trying to say 'Sandra'."

Vicki's face turned terribly pale. She slowly shook her head.

"Have you worked something out?"

"I don't know. It's impossible. Unless…" She didn't finish the sentence.

"Look," Andrew said. "We'd better get out of here. Paul and Sandra could come looking for us at any minute. The car's over there. We have to get to the police."

"I guess you're right," Vicki said.

They walked towards the car.

"Your brother," Vicki said. "What was he like?"

Andrew thought for a moment. There was no point in being tactful about someone who'd been dead for ten years.

"I don't really remember. I didn't like him, I remember that. He was tall, with dark hair and a very square chin. I thought he was cruel. He was ten years older than me. My parents doted on me – before I was born, they'd been told that my mother could never have another child – and Charles resented that. He used to pick on me all the time. When he died, I felt guilty for not liking him. I tried to forget about him."

"I don't remember him at all," Vicki said. "All I remember are the arguments. I'd be in my room, but I could hear them shouting at one another. Sandra and…"

"Your mother?"

Vicki looked embarrassed.

"I'll tell you later. You're not the only one who's been keeping a secret. Isn't that someone in the car? Who did you come with?"

Andrew turned around in alarm.

"No one."

"Have you got the keys?"

"They're in the ignition."

Andrew heard the Bentley start. Then there was a shout.

"Andrew, Vicki, get off the road. She wants to kill you!" The shouter was Paul, standing on the hillside. Before they could react, the engine ignited and the Bentley accelerated towards them. Andrew and Vicki began to run down the hill.

"Not that way!" Paul called. "She'll try to run you over!"

Andrew ran after Vicki, who was quicker than him. He glanced back. The Bentley had turned round and driven up the hill, out of sight. Maybe Sandra had realized that the game was up. She was trying to make her escape. Andrew wanted to catch Vicki up, but his body ached badly from the two falls he'd had earlier. Vicki stopped for him. They were both panting, and out of breath.

"I can't run any further," he told her.

"Why did Paul warn us?" Vicki asked.

"I don't know. Shouldn't we go and ask him?"

"No," Vicki said. "It might be a trap."

They looked around. Paul was running towards them.

"Let's go to the house," Vicki said. "She can't run us over there."

Vicki was right, but Andrew didn't really want to

go near the house again. He didn't want to go any-where. Then Paul shouted.

"She's coming back!"

"Let me help you," Vicki said.

On Vicki's arm, he limped towards the building where he had grown up, the house where his family had died. Behind them, the Bentley's engine stopped purring and began to roar.

"This way!" Vicki insisted. "Quick, by that wall!"

Andrew went where she said, glancing round as he did. The Bentley had left the road and was heading towards them. Paul ran behind it, yelling.

"Mummy, stop! Mummy!"

"Just there," Vicki said, pointing to a spot to the left of them. "That's where Daddy fell in, isn't it?"

"Yes. I think so."

"All right. Get out of the way. Behind that wall, quickly!" As the car hurtled towards them, Vicki hurried to one side, so that the driver had to choose either her or Andrew to aim at. Andrew was behind a wall, so she turned, driving the Bentley straight into Vicki. Vicki clung to one of the foundation walls. A foot in the wrong place and she would fall into the cellar. The Bentley was a well-constructed car. It would kill Vicki while the driver hardly felt a thing.

And it was coming awfully fast.

At the last moment, Vicki jumped aside, clearing the Bentley's path by centimetres. Andrew grabbed

Vicki's trembling body as the Bentley smashed into the foundation wall. They both turned to look at it. The wall shuddered and held. The driver turned to face them with a menacing, death's head stare.

"That's not Sandra," Andrew suddenly realized. "That's someone else."

The ground began to give way on the side nearest to them. As the driver undid her seat belt and grappled with the door, her side of the car tilted down until it was at a ninety-degree angle. Then the whole floor gave way. The car toppled and crashed into the cellar.

They stared down after it. Andrew could see the driver clearly. Her eyes seemed to stare into his soul with an unnatural piercing glare.

"She's not moving," Vicki said.

"That's because her neck's broken," Andrew told her.

24

Paul came running to them. He looked down at the smouldering wreck.

"Is she?"

"Yes," Vicki told him. "She is. Do you know who she was?"

Paul nodded.

"She told me her name was Sh–Charlotte," he stuttered. "She said that she was Sandra's twin sister, and my real mother. She looked like me … and Sandra. Was she telling the truth?"

"Yes," Vicki said. "She was."

Paul turned to Andrew.

"I really didn't want to hurt you," he said. "But she told me I had to. She said that you were really Andrew Partington, and your brother had done terrible things to her and Sandra and you'd do the same thing to Vicki if I didn't make you fall into the cellar. She said you deserved it. I'm sorry. She told me if I didn't she'd…" He was in tears.

"It's all right," Andrew told Paul. "I shouldn't have lied about who I was. And you helped us in the end. What made you change your mind?"

"I helped her fix the phone junction box so that she could listen in and cut it off when she wanted. She said that we had to kill Vicki, and Moira, because then we'd be safe. She'd pretend to be Sandra and look after me. I'd be the new Lord Hetherington."

"Moira?" Vicki said, urgently. "Is Moira still alive?"

"She is," Paul told them. "She's locked up in the butterfly room. Charlotte went down there just before we came after you. She said she had to do something with the generator."

"Oh, God," Vicki said. "We've got to get back there."

"What is it?" Andrew said to her. "What's wrong?"

"Don't you see? She wants to destroy the evidence. She's going to destroy the Hall the same way that she destroyed Partington House. She doesn't care about the Hall, only about the title for Paul."

"Is she really Sandra's twin?"

"Yes. I was going to tell you, but … there's no

time to explain now. She'll have set the generator to overload and removed the safety valve."

"How do you know all this?" Andrew asked.

"Because that's what she did before – to your family. I'm sorry. I thought she was dead. Daddy said she'd killed herself, not long after it happened. He made us all promise not to talk about her, for Paul's sake, he said. If I'd known…" She stopped speaking. Paul was tugging at her sleeve.

"Come on," he said, "we've got to go!"

"Wait!" Andrew said. "I can hardly walk. Surely it's all right. There's hardly any oil left."

"There doesn't have to be that much fuel," Vicki said.

Behind them, there was a loud bang. For a moment, Andrew thought it was Hetherington Hall. Then he turned round and saw that it was the Bentley. Flames poured out of the hole in the ground. Thick black smoke filled the air.

"Like I said," Vicki repeated. "It doesn't need that much fuel."

"You and Paul will have to go without me," Andrew told her.

"I don't want to leave you."

"I'll be all right. Take care."

Paul and Vicki left, no longer brother and sister, but aunt and nephew.

Andrew sat on the driveway to what had once been his family home, trying to think. He seemed to have discovered what he had set out to find: Vicki's elder sister, Charlotte, had caused the death of his father, mother and brother. He still didn't know why. But he was nearly there. Vicki, it seemed, knew the answer. Maybe, if he had told the truth from the start, she wouldn't have kept back the story of Sandra's twin sister. By now, four more people were dead and, unless Vicki was very swift, a fifth would die too. What could have happened ten years ago to set these terrible events in motion?

A car hooted and he looked up. It was Vicki's brown Mini, driving down the winding road into the valley. The car drove up to where he sat and the driver got out, smiling cheerfully. It was Alice, her blonde hair blowing in the breeze. She looked so lovely that Andrew thought she was a mirage. Alice smiled at him, then stared at the smoke. Finally, her eyes rested on Andrew's tattered clothes.

"I saw the smoke," she said. "What's going on?"

"Over now," he muttered. Aching and exhausted, Andrew couldn't get any more words out. Alice pointed at the car.

"I found this parked on the side of the road a mile from our house with the keys left in it. Your stuck-up girlfriend ran out of petrol, did she?"

Andrew nodded.

"When she didn't come back for it, I put a couple of gallons in and decided to drive it over. Then I saw the smoke and made a detour."

She took a breath, and looked around.

"What happened?" she asked.

"Can I tell you later?" Andrew asked. "It's a big relief to see you."

"You look like you need some help."

"I can hardly walk," Andrew admitted.

"I'll get you into the car."

Alice put her arms beneath his shoulders and helped him up. For someone so slender, she was surprisingly strong.

"Lean on me," she said, and he did. Then she added, "Where's Vicki? She didn't start that fire over there, did she?"

Andrew's brain suddenly came back to life.

"We have to drive to Hetherington Hall *now*, as quickly as possible," he insisted. "There's someone there in terrible danger."

Alice looked at him as though he was mad.

"Please," Andrew said. "Trust me."

Alice stared at him for a few seconds, weighing the situation up.

"All right," she said, as Andrew squirmed un-comfortably into the passenger seat, "let's go."

Andrew hardly said a word to Alice once he was in the car. She was driving – and talking – very quickly indeed.

"You're Andrew Partington, aren't you? My mum recognized you when you came round on Friday. She used to clean at your house."

"Did she?"

"She said you wouldn't remember. But Mum couldn't understand why you didn't know that Sandra Hetherington was going to marry your brother."

"I was away at school when it all happened."

Alice nodded. She was keeping her eyes on the road, and didn't turn round to see the fascination with which Andrew received the information she was giving him.

"It was terrible," Alice said. "You must have had an awful time. People still talk about it. What happened to the sister?"

"Which sister?"

"Charlotte. The one they say did it. 'The mad twins', my Mum used to call Sandra and Charlotte. They were both in love with the same bloke – your brother. But presumably you know all this already?"

Andrew bit his tongue.

"Not all of it. I never came back here, not even for the funeral. The aunt who looked after me thought that I was too young to understand."

"Everyone round here reckons that Charlotte burnt your old house down. But it was covered up, wasn't it? They put Charlotte in some loony bin – that's what people say – though some reckon that Sandra's the really loopy one. Is all that true?"

"I don't know," Andrew told Alice. "But I think so."

They were coming up to the hall. Andrew checked his watch. Vicki and Paul were coming the shorter way, over the fields, but they wouldn't have had time to get here yet.

"Don't park too close," Andrew told Alice. "There might be danger."

"Danger?" she said, getting out of the car. "Look, Andrew, I like you. I want to help you. But you're acting as though you're in shock or something. What's going on?"

"The Hall might be about to catch fire. I'm going in."

Alice looked at him, presumably to check if he was frothing at the mouth. Then she helped him out of his seat.

"Why are you going in, if it's dangerous?"

"Because Moira's trapped down in the cellar."

Alice gave him another hard look.

"If she's really in the cellar, than I'd better go for her. You can barely walk."

"I'm going in too."

"Come on then, if you can."

Andrew could hardly object to Alice helping him. He didn't want to put her life at risk, but he couldn't save Moira on his own, either. Alice rushed ahead. He could barely keep up with her.

"Where in the cellar?" she asked, as they went into the hall.

"The butterfly room. A right turn at the end."

She got to the top of the cellar steps and opened the door. There was a deafening clanking noise.

"It's hot," she shouted, before going down. "You know, I wouldn't do this if it was anyone other than Moira. She's the only person here who ever treated me decently."

Andrew followed as closely as he could. There were sparks coming from the generator. The key to the butterfly room was, thankfully, in the lock. He heard Alice going into the room. She came out again just as he was getting to the bottom of the steps.

"I need your help," she told him. "Moira's really weak and dehydrated. She can hardly walk."

Andrew joined Alice in the butterfly room. It smelt rank and airless. Moira was panting. She had lost a lot of weight. Andrew worked out that she must have been in there for three days.

"Wait," Moira whispered as they lifted her between them. She pointed to one of the wooden drawers on the table.

"There's no time to save butterflies," Andrew said.

"Not butterflies," she whispered.

He reached for the drawer and looked in it. There were clippings and torn pages. The drawer concealed the pages which had been torn from the house books – the hidden history of Hetherington Hall. Andrew picked them up and stuffed them into his jacket.

"Come on," Alice said.

The buzzing noise from the generator intensified as they carried Moira along the corridor. Andrew could hardly climb the steps himself, never mind help Moira. Somehow, with Alice pushing from behind, they all got into the hall.

The noise from below grew louder as the pressure in the oil drum mounted. Andrew realized that what he was hearing now would have been the last sound which his parents and brother heard before they died.

"Move!" Alice exhorted. "Move!"

They burst through the door into sudden sunshine. As they stumbled down the steps, Andrew saw Vicki and Paul running across the fields towards them.

"Stay back! Stay back!" Alice shouted.

The explosion blew out all of the windows on all three floors. Dirty glass showered Andrew, Alice and Moira, cutting what skin they had exposed. Andrew kept moving until they got to the car. Then, as flames engulfed the house, they sheltered behind it. Paul and Vicki joined them.

"Are you all right?" Vicki asked the housekeeper, hugging her.

"I am now, my dear. I am now."

25

Mr Gallagher, the Hetherington family solicitor, met Andrew, Alice, Vicki, Moira and Paul at the police station. He spoke to Andrew.

"I knew your parents," he said. "They were good people."

Andrew reached into one of his pockets and handed the solicitor the envelope containing the will.

"Have you read this?" the solicitor asked.

Andrew shook his head. Mr Gallagher got out the papers and looked through them for several minutes.

"I see. I see," he muttered to himself.

A Detective Inspector came in and spoke to Mr Gallagher.

"I spoke to Dr Rutherford, as you suggested.

She confirmed that Charlotte Hetherington was released into the community last month. When Charlotte didn't get in touch with her social worker, Dr Rutherford contacted Hetherington Hall, with some difficulty. She says that she has spoken to you and to Charlotte's sister."

"Did she tell you that Charlotte had been released?" Andrew asked Mr Gallagher.

"Yes," he admitted. "The Doctor said that Charlotte was mentally stable, showed no interest in returning to her family, and had been found a placement in the south of England. I told Lord Hetherington this and, as a result, he made a small provision for her in his new will."

Then the solicitor picked up the document and read from it.

"And to my eldest daughter, Charlotte, I leave £10,000, on condition that she does not seek to have contact with the new Lord Hetherington."

He put the papers down.

"However, the new will has no legal weight, because Lord Hetherington died before it could be witnessed. Moreover, this will assumes that Lord Hetherington has the proceeds from the sale of Hetherington Hall. He intended to make adequate provision for each of his daughters. He meant to pay off his debts, buy a modest house, and live off the interest from his capital. When he died, the capital would have been divided equally between Paul,

Sandra and Victoria, apart from bequests to Charlotte and Moira." He turned to the housekeeper.

"There is a bequest to you in the old will, Moira, but I don't know if there'll be the cash to cover it. Does anyone know if his insurance policies were up to date?"

"They were," Andrew told them.

"In that case, there should be enough to pay off the debts. You might have some money to see you through college, Vicki. Things will be more difficult for Paul."

"I'll look after Paul," Vicki promised.

"I'll help you, dear," Moira said.

"I'm sure that Andrew will help as well," Mr Gallagher told the others. "After all, he is Paul's uncle."

Andrew had already worked most of this out, but the situation still felt very strange. Only this morning, his nephew had tried to kill him. Mr Gallagher turned to Andrew again.

"Do you know the full story of what happened?"

"Nearly. It all started with my brother, Charles, I think."

The solicitor nodded.

"Charles was a feckless young man. Officially, he was Sandra's boyfriend, but he was secretly seeing Charlotte, too. The girls were near identical twins, but had very different personalities. Finally, Charles decided to marry Sandra, but still slept with

Charlotte from time to time. Sandra suspected, and complained, but Charlotte was the dominant of the twins, and a convincing liar. Shortly before the marriage was due to take place, Charlotte discovered that she was pregnant. She must have told Charles, but no one knows how he reacted. My guess is that he told Charlotte that he wanted nothing further to do with her. The following night, Charlotte tampered with the generator at the Partington house, causing it to explode.

"Charlotte was found to be unfit to stand trial. The case was kept out of the papers, but the story was common knowledge, and the Hetheringtons stopped moving in society from that date. They had Charlotte committed to a home, where her pregnancy was kept a close secret. Shortly after her committal, Sandra and Vicki were told that Charlotte had killed herself. They had no reason to disbelieve their parents."

He lowered his voice.

"I was – against my better judgement – drawn into the secret. After the twins, Lady Hetherington could bear no more children. Lord Hetherington longed for a male heir. When a scan showed that Charlotte was carrying a male child, he determined to pass it off as his own. Lady Hetherington went away, claiming to be pregnant. When the baby was born, Charlotte was told that it was being adopted. In fact, a friendly doctor falsified a birth certificate, describing Lord and Lady Hetherington as the parents.

"Unfortunately, it now seems that Charlotte realized what had been done. On her release from hospital, she came straight to Hetherington Hall, and set about getting revenge for herself and assuring her son of his inheritance. She must have sabotaged the heater in the bathroom – it didn't matter who was killed, she wanted to get everyone, except her son Paul, whom she warned."

"She came into my room at night," Paul interrupted, in a shrill voice. "At first, I thought she was Sandra. She was really nice to me. I'd get her food and stuff. You saw her, Andrew, the night when you stayed in my room."

He started crying again.

"I never wanted to hurt anyone, but she said we had to. We *had* to."

"It's all right," Vicki hugged him. "It's all right."

The solicitor continued.

"We don't know how Charlotte killed Sandra. I suspect that she forced her to put on the wedding dress, then stabbed her. Sandra was physically strong, but frequently deranged since Charles died. And Charlotte could always twist Sandra around her little finger.

"The other deaths you know about. I surmise that, by killing Lord Hetherington, Charlotte hoped to ensure that her son became the next Lord

Hetherington. She would pose as Sandra and, between them, they would inherit everything. But her actions had the opposite effect. The house, having burnt down, cannot be sold. It was, I'm sad to say, badly underinsured. And the deception about Paul's parentage has to end here, too. There's bound to be publicity. As a bastard grandson, he cannot inherit."

Vicki looked perturbed.

"It's me, then," she said, with a grimace. "I'm the only one left."

"What does that make her?" Andrew asked. "A baroness?"

"I'm afraid not," Mr Gallagher told her. "This will be a shock, Victoria, but you, too, are illegitimate. Lady Hetherington was not your mother."

Vicki's eyes nearly popped out of their sockets. Mr Gallagher continued.

"As I explained earlier – after the birth of the twins, Lady Hetherington could bear no more children. Your father was – as I'm sure you're aware – a promiscuous man. Your mother was one of his mistresses. He and Lady Hetherington did formally adopt you, but, as I'm sure you're aware, adopted children cannot inherit a title." He paused, then added, "I'm sorry."

Vicki was in shock.

"I never wanted a title," she said. "But you say, my mother ... wasn't my real mother?"

"No."

"Then ... who is?"

The Detective Inspector came back in.

"We're ready to take the statements now."

Mr Gallagher got up.

"If I could have a brief word outside first, Inspector. There are one or two things I'd like to clear up."

The solicitor went out with the policeman. When Andrew looked back at Vicki, she and Moira were holding each other's hands.

"Why do you think I stayed with the family all those years?" Moira was asking. "I told your mother that they could only adopt you if I was allowed to stay. She didn't like it, but she put up with it. Then, when they found you were a girl ... she never loved you like I did. I couldn't leave."

Mother and daughter sobbed in each other's arms.

Andrew, Alice and Paul left the room quietly, giving the two women some privacy.

"The ambulance has arrived," Mr Gallagher told Andrew. "Is there anything else you want me to tell you before they take you to hospital?"

"I think I know the full story," Andrew told him. "But there is one thing I'm curious about. What happens to the title now?"

Mr Gallagher frowned.

"If Charlotte had lived, it would have been hers, no matter what her crimes, because she would have been Lord Hetherington's only surviving legitimate child. As it is, the title falls into abeyance. If no legitimate heir can be found, then…" The solicitor made a gesture like a puff of smoke disappearing.

"Perhaps," he added, "that would be the most appropriate ending."